Evelyn Everett-Green

Pat

The Lighthouse Boy

Evelyn Everett-Green

Pat
The Lighthouse Boy

ISBN/EAN: 9783337254971

Printed in Europe, USA, Canada, Australia, Japan

Cover: Foto ©Andreas Hilbeck / pixelio.de

More available books at **www.hansebooks.com**

Pat

The Lighthouse Boy.

BY

E. EVERETT-GREEN,

AUTHOR OF

"EUSTACE MARCHMONT;" "WINNING THE VICTORY;"
"TEMPLE'S TRIAL;" ETC. ETC.

NEW YORK:

WARD & DRUMMOND.

CONTENTS

LIST OF ILLUSTRATIONS

PAT
THE LIGHTHOUSE BOY

CHAPTER I

LONE ROCK LIGHTHOUSE

MOTHER, mother, mother!" cried Pat, drawing a long breath of awe and wonder, "it seems like as if we had gone straight to heaven!"

"Nay, my son, not quite to heaven, for sure the blessed book tells us that there will be no more sea there;" and the woman looked out over the heaving expanse of grey-blue water with a strange soft wistfulness in her big grey eyes. One would have said to look at her then that she had known what it meant to lose those near and dear to her through the hungry cruel sea, as indeed in her young life she had done; for she was an Irish woman, and had lived all her young life beside the wild coast of Galway, and many of those who bore her name had found a last resting-place beneath the heaving tossing waves. Therefore it was small wonder if she had come to look forward to that bright land beyond the moaning waves, of which it has been expressly said that " there shall be no more sea."

But Patrick could scarcely enter at this moment into his mother's feelings on this score. He was wild with excitement and delight, as indeed he well might be, seeing that he had only just come from a close crowded alley in a smelling fishing and trading town to this lighthouse home, which seemed to lie alone in the very heart of the sea, with nothing above or around but sea and sky, the wild sea-birds for visitors, and the plash of the waves for one long " hush-a-by." No wonder if in these first moments of returning consciousness to outward things, little Pat felt as though some strange thing, almost like death, had befallen him, and that he had awakened to find himself either in heaven itself, or else in some beautiful and wonderful place very like to it indeed.

For Pat had been very ill. He had been a frail little fellow all his short life, and had never been able to run about and shout and play as the other children did who lived in his court. He had spent most of his time indoors with his mother, growing more and more wan and white with each succeeding summer as it came and went. Although the sea lay only a mile away from his home, he had scarcely ever walked as far as its margin, for there was nothing to attract him when he did so. It was not beautiful open sea such as what he was now looking upon, but a piece of ugly tidal water, with quays and wharfs lining the brink, and evil smells everywhere.

His father had a boat, and would have taken his boy out with him in it sometimes ; but Pat was afraid of the rough looks of the other men, and his mother knew that the frail child would be weary to death long before he could be put ashore. So that Pat had grown up seeing little more than the sights of his own court, hearing little besides the shouts and cries and foul words so freely bandied about there. He had not been much better off in that respect than if he had come from a London slum, and this sudden awakening in the Lone Rock Lighthouse was like an awakening in a new world.

It was on Pat's account that his parents had come to this strange new home. When the hot May sunshine had come streaming into the alley in which the child had been reared, he had suddenly failed and fallen ill of a low fever, which had almost sapped his little life away; and so near had he come to the gates of death, that the doctor had shaken his head and said, "There is only one thing that can save him, and that is lots of fresh air and sunshine and pure salt breezes—not the breezes you get in here, reeking with all that is foul and impure. If you keep him here, he will die. The only chance for him is to take him right away; and I am afraid that, situated as you are, you will find it impossible to do so."

Perhaps it would have been impossible at another time; but just at this very juncture it chanced that Lone Rock Lighthouse was vacant, and indeed the post of caretaker had actually been offered to Nathaniel Carey, because he was known to be a steady respectable man, who could be relied upon to do his duty there. Lone Rock Lighthouse was always changing its keeper, for the life there was so solitary that men could not long stand the strain of it; and by the end of a year, or a couple of years, almost always resigned the post, in spite of the regular pay and comfortable home.

It was not a post that Nat would have cared to accept under ordinary circumstances, for he was a sociable man, and liked to have other men about him; but when the life of his only child was at stake, and his wife, with wan drawn face and piteous eyes, pointed to the little figure on the bed and told him what the doctor had said, the only thing to be done was to go and accept the post without any more hesitation; and the next business was to get the sick child removed there upon the first calm and suitable day.

For Lone Rock was not to be approached at all times and seasons, even in summer weather, and often was cut off from communication with the shore in winter for many weeks together. It was built upon a very dangerous sunken reef, round which the sea boiled and surged and raged from year's end to year's end. And herein lay the chief peril and the chief drawback of the keeper's life. If anything were to go

wrong with him or with his home—if he were to
be ill, or in want of some necessary of life, or if
the structure of the lighthouse needed attention,
it might be long weary days, or even weeks,
before he could receive the help he had signalled
for. It is true that every precaution was taken
to ensure his safety. The structure was carefully examined by competent persons at short
intervals. A large store of dried and salted
provisions was always kept under the roof of the
building, so that the keeper and his assistant
might never be put to actual shifts for food, and
stores of oil, for the great lamp, were likewise
kept—stores which could scarcely run out, however long a spell of bad weather might last.
Every care and precaution was taken; but for
all that the life there was one of singular isola-
tion, and men had been known to go mad
during the long dreary winter months; and
once a terrible crime had been committed there
through this very cause—a crime of which men
whispered still sometimes with 'bated breath,
though Pat's mother always resolved that the
child should never hear the gruesome tale.

Eileen Carey was the first woman who had had
the courage to make a home upon the Lone

Rock. Other keepers had either been un-married men, or had left their wives behind for the time that they lived there. But Nat Carey came with his wife and his child; and those in authority were glad that it was so, for they argued that a man who had a real home about him would not suffer from the loneliness of the life as others had done; and they had done several things to brighten up the little home before the new-comers arrived there. Eileen's clever hands had done more so soon as they were fairly landed, for little Pat required very little nursing, as he lay day after day in a trance of weakness and exhaustion. But his mother was satisfied that each day he grew slightly stronger, and was quite content to wait until he should awaken to a knowledge of his new surroundings, which she meantime strove to make as bright and as homelike as possible; for she meant that her husband and her little boy should not lack any of the comforts which her hands could pro-vide during their whole stay on the Lone Rock.

And now the mother was to have her re-ward. For several days Pat had begun to look about him, to follow her movements with his eyes, to answer when she spoke to him, and to smile when she looked his way. He was a long time in taking notice of anything except his mother and father. It seemed to them as though he had no eyes for any of the other strange things about him. He must have known that this new room, with its whitewashed walls, so spotless and clean, its queer shape, its fresh furniture and bright curtains to the sunny window, was not the room in which he had lived for all the previous years of his small life. Yet he did not take any open notice of these things for many days, and his mother would not let him be spoken to about them, for, as she truly said, if he hadn't strength to take them in with his eyes, he had far better be let alone till the strength began to come back to him of itself.

And now that time had come. Pat had for some days been noticing everything—noticing with an ever-increasing curiosity and pleasure. He had begun by asking what was "that funny noise that never stopped;" and when his mother had told him it was the sound of the waves, he had asked "how they got there, for they didn't use to be so near." And so little by little Eileen had told him all the tale—how father had been offered the care of Lone Rock Lighthouse, and

how the doctor had said that little Pat might
thrive and grow strong if he were to be taken
right away from the court in which he had
always lived. And Pat lay and smiled at the
tale, and got his mother to tell it him again and
again, and grew so fond of the song of the sea
before ever he had been able to get up and look
at it, that he often told her "it was making him
well as fast as it could;" and she would smile
with tears in her eyes and believe him.

Every day had seen some improvement in
little Pat's condition; but it seemed long to the
mother before he had expressed the wish to get
up and look out at the window. She knew that
would be the first thing he was likely to ask for,
because he lay and watched the sunny square
hour after hour, with a smile of contentment on
his face. But it was only to-day that he had
said he wanted to get up and look; and now
she was sitting with him wrapped in a blanket,
he standing with his little bare feet upon the
window-seat, and gazing with wide-open wondering eyes over the vast expanse of sparkling
water that was as little like "the sea," as he
had been accustomed to think of it, as was
the noise of the waves like the ceaseless bawling

B

and brawling that his ears had grown used to
in the court whence he had come.

Pat was greatly moved and excited by all
he saw, and from that day forward was most
eager and anxious to regain his strength, that
he might be able to explore the wonders of the
lighthouse, and see what manner of place his
new home was. So he ate everything that
his mother brought to him " to make him
strong ; " he slept from sunset till morning like
a young bird. He began to chatter and laugh
to his father whenever he appeared ; and long
before he could attempt to mount the giddy
spiral staircase, which led to the big circular
room where the great lamp lived, he got his
father to tell him all about it, and at night
he would get out of bed if he chanced to wake
up to see the circle of flashing light which it
cast around upon the dark heaving mass of
waters. The child was fascinated by the thought
of the great lamp's lonely vigil over the wide
empty sea long before he was able to understand
what it was that it was doing.

The first step in the child's convalescence
which seemed to mark the era of " getting
better," was when he was able to be dressed and

to go into the other room for his meals. The base of the lighthouse was divided into several queer-shaped rooms. There was the sleeping-room, in which the child had hitherto spent all his time; and opening from that was the kitchen or living room, in which he was used to hear his mother bustling about as he lay in bed. There were also, as he presently found out, other smaller and darker chambers. One of these was appropriated to the use of the keeper's assistant, whilst others contained the stores for the lamp and its caretakers, of which mention has been made before. It was quite a surprise to Pat to learn that he and his parents were not the only occupants of the lighthouse. He had never heard any strange voice from the inner room all the time he had been lying in bed, and so he was very much astonished the first day he sat up to supper, to see a heavy-looking dark-browed man come slouching in, and taking his seat without a word of explanation or apology. The child looked wonderingly at his mother.

"That is Jim," she said; "Jim helps daddy with the lamp. They take it in turns to watch. Jim, this is our little boy, Pat—him as has been so ill, you know. I have told you about him often."

Pat looked across the table and nodded, but Jim said nothing, and scarcely appeared to hear himself addressed. He took his food in perfect silence, and as soon as he had finished he got up and went out, and they heard him going heavily up the winding staircase towards the lantern house.

"Can't he talk?" asked Pat wonderingly. "Is he dumb, do you think?" Eileen smiled, and shook her head at the question.

"Nay, he can speak. He has a tongue, but he is wonderful loth to use it. I suppose it is the life here as has made him so quiet. Surly Jim is what folks call him. He has been with several keepers, but none has had a good word for him, save that he does his work well and can be trusted with the lamp. He won't be keeper, though they did offer him the place. But he stays on year after year when nobody else will. He does all his work well, and is very clean and neat; but he scarce opens his lips, save in the way of business, from one year's end to the other."

This seemed so very strange to Pat that he sat for some time turning it over in his mind. He thought when he had time he would try and get Surly Jim to talk to him; but at present there were many other things to think of, and the child's head was crowded with new ideas and questions.

What a fascinating place the lighthouse was! As he grew stronger, he began to explore it from end to end, and found new wonders every hour of the day.

There was the little door leading out to the rocks on which the place was built, and the flight of slippery steps which led down to the tiny creek where the boat lay moored. There were chains for hauling up the boat in rough weather on to a ledge, where it would not be likely to be swept away, save perhaps in the very worst weather; and at low tide there was a wonderful mass of rock uncovered by the sea, where he could wander about and pick up untold treasures, such as he had never seen or dreamed of before. And his mother was not afraid to let him wander about here. She had grown up herself on the wild coast, and had no fear of the slippery rocks and the plashing waves. Pat was only instructed to take off shoes and stockings before trying to scramble about them, and very soon he grew so sure-footed and fearless that neither parent was afraid for him. Moreover, he was growing brown and healthy-looking, and stronger than he had ever been in his life before ; and though he might not be very robust for some time to come, he was gaining every day, and they were glad and thankful to see it.

Oh, that wide, wild, beautiful sea! How Pat came to love it! It was at once a friend and playmate and a deep unspeakable mystery. He was never tired of watching its wild play over the rocks, or of sitting listening to its deep strange voice, as it laughed or shouted in its wild wonderful strength. He would sit with his face towards the west as the sun was going down, and watch whilst the great blazing ball dipped lower and lower, till it sank, sank, sank, right into the sea itself. And then as the sea opened its mouth and swallowed it up, it seemed all dyed crimson and gold, as though it had caught some of the colour from the prisoner it had taken.

The child would watch with awe this daily mystery, and when he found that every morning the sun came up again out of the sea, but in quite a different place, he was awed and perplexed past the power of speech. It never occurred to him to ask questions even of his mother about this daily wonder; but he watched it with unfailing interest, and seemed to drink in new thoughts every time it happened. He was more and more sure that his new home was very like heaven—not so beautiful as the real heaven, because Jesus would be there to make the light of it: but like it in some things—in its peace and beauty and wonderful calm. Pat had been so near to the gates of death that his mind naturally turned to thoughts like this. He was still not strong enough to play more than a few hours every day, and the rest of his time would be spent sitting on the rocks or at the window watching the sea, and thinking about it, until his face took a new expression, as though some of the sunshine and the clearness of the blue sea had got into them and had taken up an abode there.

Very often he would carry out his little Testament to his favourite nooks in the rocks, and find some of the places where he loved to read. He was particularly fond of the chapter about the "sea of glass mingled with fire," because he was so sure it must be just like his own sea at sunset time; and there were other places he

was fond of too, because they always set him
thinking and dreaming, and chimed in with all
his new ideas. He did not talk much about
his thoughts; when he went in to his mother
he would chatter to her of his play and of the
live things he had seen in the pools. To his
father he would ask questions about the lamp,
and how it kept awake all the night through—
whether it never went to sleep by accident; for
to him that lamp was like a living creature.
He had only seen it once, because the climb up
the spiral stairs turned him queer and giddy,
and his parents had bidden him wait till he was
stronger before he tried again. But that one
visit had been enough to excite him strangely,
and he always thought with awe of the great
revolving light going round and round the whole
night through. He was never tired of hearing
about it and asking questions; but of his own
strange thoughts, when he was all alone with
the sea and the sunshine, he said nothing. That
was his own secret—perhaps because he lacked
words in which to express himself. And the
new, strange, beautiful life began for little Pat
upon the isolated reef which supported Lone
Rock Lighthouse.

CHAPTER II

"SURLY JIM"

ONE night, contrary to his usual habit, Pat could not sleep. He had been to sleep for some hours during the early part of the night, but now he was wide awake, and he did not feel like going to sleep any more. He sat up in bed, and looked round him in the moonlight. There were his father and mother, both sleeping calmly and quietly. If father was in bed, Jim must be up in the lighthouse, watching to see the big lamp did not "go to sleep by accident," as the child phrased it in his own mind. He was suddenly taken with a vivid curiosity to go to that lighted chamber himself. He had only been there by day as yet. He wondered what it would look like at night; and almost before he knew what he was doing, he had slipped out of bed, and

was putting on his clothes. He did not want
to disturb his father, who would by-and-by
have to get up and take his own watch in the
tower, as the child called it in his thoughts, so
he moved softly about, and presently found
himself creeping up the dim staircase that was
lighted at intervals by small lamps placed in
niches in the wall.

It made him rather breathless to mount so
many stairs, but curiosity and a love of adventure led him on, and presently he found himself
within the wonderful chamber he had visited
before, only that now the great bright lamp
with its myriad wicks and wonderful reflectors
was alight, and slowly moving round and round,
so that at one time it showed a red eye to those
out at sea in great ships, at another a green,
and again a pure white light, as white as crystal.

The child stood gazing at the wonderful
mechanism without speaking a word. He was
trying to see how it moved, and by what power
the great reflectors moved round and round.
Of course he could not understand, and he
quickly came to the conclusion that the thing
was some great living monster, and that it had
to be watched all the night through lest it went

to sleep, or refused to do its part properly.
He wondered, with a thrill of nervous terror,
whether it would resent his intrusion into its
special domain. Standing as he did in the full
glare of the light, he could not hope to escape
observation, and he looked about him as if for
a hiding-place in case of attack.

And then his eye fell upon the figure of the
solitary watcher—a bent bowed figure, in a
slouching and indifferent attitude, now quite
familiar to the child, although he and the
individual who owned that rough exterior had
never as yet exchanged a single word.

Pat was not a shy child as a rule, but he had
always stood in awe of "Surly Jim." He could
eat better and chatter more freely when the man
was not present at table. He shrank a little
into himself always when Jim entered the living
room. It was not often that he did this, save
when called to meals, for when not on duty, he
was either sleeping in his own room, or sitting
in the boat smoking a short black pipe, and Pat
had never attempted to approach him at these
times. Now he was nearer to him than he had
ever been, except at table, and yet the man
appeared to take no manner of notice of his

approach. He sat with his elbows on his knees, and his head in his hands, and did not seem to look up at the child's cautious approach. Pat felt certain he had been seen, but this indifference seemed a little uncanny. He drew near step by step, and at last laid one small cold hand on the knee of the assistant.

"Is it alive?" he asked softly, divided in his awe of the wonderful mechanism and its grim watcher. The man slowly lifted his head, and stared at the child without attempting to speak. Pat hesitated a moment, and then climbed upon the bench upon which Jim was seated, and slipped his small thin hand within the horny palm of the man. He felt that he must have hold of something human up here in this strange place of light and movement. He was trembling, and yet he was not exactly afraid.

His hand was suffered to remain where he had placed it. Jim glanced furtively down at the small fingers in his hard hand, and perhaps something of an unwonted nature stole into his heart, for, to the astonishment of the child, he suddenly spoke.

"What did you want to know, little master?"

Now Pat thought it was very grand to be

addressed as "little master," and his opinion of Jim began quickly to change. He could not be as cross as he tried to make out. The child took courage, and went on with his questions, in the order in which they came into his mind.

"Is it alive?" he asked, with his eyes upon the slowly moving reflectors, as they solemnly revolved round and round the centre light.

"Seems like as if she was," answered the man; "her takes a deal of food, and a deal of cleaning, and a deal of watching. Her be as full of moods as wimmin folk mostly be. She can't get along without a deal of notice, no more than they can!"

Pat fixed his wondering eyes on the speaker's face. He was almost as much fascinated in Jim's slow and deliberate speech as in the subject in hand. It was almost as though the mouth of the dumb had been unstopped, as though it was only in this strange place, and in the witching hour of night, that the man's tongue was unloosed. He spoke very slowly, as though it was not easy for him to find words in which to clothe his thoughts.

"It's a *she* then, is it?" asked Pat, all alive in a moment. "That's very interesting. I

always thought she must be alive, but mother
and father laugh at me. Perhaps they don't
know so well as you—you've been here so much
longer, haven't you?"

"I've been a-keeping of her this five years or
more," said Jim, after a long pause, in which
Pat began to wonder whether he would ever
speak again or not; "afore that I was in prison.
They let me come out to look after her. It was
so hard to get anybody to stop."

Pat felt a thrill of awe run through him. He
had heard of people going to prison of course,
and had known many lads and men who had
passed through the ordeal of going there for a
time; but that seemed different from Jim's case.
He wondered whether this strange gruff man
had ever been a murderer, or had done some
very dreadful deed. If so, was it safe to be
sitting up here with him in the night, all alone?
Might he not perhaps think it would be a good
opportunity for throwing him down the staircase, or out over the gallery into the sea? For
a moment the child felt a queer sensation of
fear come over him, and then it all passed
away as fast as it came, for Jim still held him
by the hand, and his clasp upon his fingers felt

kind and friendly. He looked up into the
sullen, weather-beaten face above him with his
confiding smile, and asked—

"What had they put you in prison for?
Had you done anything bad?"

"No," answered Jim, after the inevitable
pause, "I hadn't. It were another man; but
they wouldn't believe it. He gave evidence
against me, and they took his word, not mine.
Folks said it were proved against I, and so I
was sent to prison. But I hadn't done it—I
don't care what they say."

"No, and I don't care, either!" cried Pat,
with hot partisanship; "I know you didn't do
it! It was they who were wicked and bad to
send you to prison! But they had to let you
out again, you see!"

He spoke the last words with an air as of
triumph, edging up towards Jim in a confidential
way as he did so. The man was knitting his
heavy brows, and looking as though he was not
sure whether all this were not a strange dream.

"They let me out to come here. I had three
more years to run. They said if I would stop
and do my duty it should count as though I had
served my time. So I came, and here I be.

It's the only home I've known since *that* thing
happened, and I don't want no other. I've got
fond of *her*"—nodding towards the big lamp;
" she looks kind at me now, and she's the
only friend I've got. I'll bide here as long as
I live. It's sore work going back to find all
one's mates dead or changed to you."

" Yes; don't go back," said Pat; " stay here
with us. I'll be your friend, too. I should
like a friend of my own. Father and mother
don't count like that, because they *are* just
father and mother. I should like to have a
friend as well. Let us be friends, Jim ; and
perhaps then *she'll* let me be her friend too."

Pat spoke in the simplest good faith, whilst
Jim passed his hand across his eyes, and then
looked down at the small figure beside him,
rather as though he were not sure that it was
not all a dream after all. Pat was not altogether
sure of this either. It was certainly very queer
to be up in the middle of the night just under
the great lamp, sitting hand in hand with Jim
and talking about being friends. He looked
up into the rough face above him and smiled
as he said—

" Jim, do you think we are *both* dreaming?"

" Jim opened a door close by." —*Page* 35.

C

"It seems almost like it, little master,'
answered the man; "but we'll go out into the
gallery, and get a breath of fresh air. That's
the best thing to wake one up if one is getting
be-fogged."

Pat was delighted at this notion. He knew
that there was an outside gallery running all
round the glass house where the lamp lived.
He had seen it from the boat when his father
had rowed him out a little way in the evenings;
but he had never been out on it before, and to
go there at night for the first time seemed a very
wonderful thing to do. He would see how the
sea looked from up there in the moonlight;
and perhaps Jim would be able to tell him how
the sun managed to swim round from one side
to the other before morning, and why it always
came up in just the same place every day, and
went down in the same place every night. Jim
must know a lot of things, living so much up
there, he thought.

So Jim got up and opened a door close
by, and a breath of cold wind came rushing
into the warm room under the big lamp. Pat
looked wonderingly out into the black darkness,
and shivered a little, holding Jim's hand fast in

his small tenacious clasp. And then Jim, all in a moment, shuffled somehow out of his warm rough pilot coat, and wrapped it round the child's thin frame, and lifting him bodily in his strong arms, carried him out into the still calm night, shutting the door behind him as he went, that the draught might not make the lamp flicker or flare.

For a moment it came into the child's head to wonder whether Jim was going to throw him over the gallery rail and into the sea, and he shut his eyes tight, and breathed a little prayer. But something in the strong clasp in which he was held stilled this fear almost before it had taken shape, and the next minute the child wonderingly opened his eyes and gazed with awe at the scene before him.

It did not seem dark now, for the silver moon rode high in the sky, and though the sea beneath looked black in places, there was a great track of silver light right across it where the moonlight lay, and sometimes a white sea-bird would fly athwart the silver track, and for that moment its beautiful white wings seemed to shine like silver too. The little plashing waves below were tipped and crested with phosphorescent light, and broke against the reef in a thousand ripples of molten silver. The whole world seemed as if it had been turned into ebony and silver, and the child looked and looked, drinking in the wonderful beauty, which was beyond his powers of comprehension.

He forgot all the questions he had meant to ask ; he forgot the puzzle about the sun and its setting and rising ; he could think of nothing but the strange majestic beauty of the summer night, and looking up into Jim's dark face, he wondered if it looked the same to him.

He was beautifully snug and warm wrapped up, and held close and safely. There was nothing to mar his happiness and wonder. He gazed, and gazed, and gazed again, till at last his confused thoughts found vent in words.

" I can't think how He thought of it ! "

" Who thought of what, little master ? " asked Jim, who had now found his tongue, and did not seem indisposed to use it more freely.

" Why, God to be sure," answered the child reverently. " You know that God made everything; and before He made it He'd have to think of it, and know what it would look like ; and I can't think how He did ! "

" I don't seem to know much about that,"
said the man, as Pat looked up at him as if for
a suggestion.   " It's a many years since I heard
the name of God spoke—except to swear by,"
he added as an afterthought.

Now Pat knew very well what swearing
sounded like, for he had heard a great deal too
much of it in his small life.   But his mother
had always taught him to shun those people
who used bad words, and he had never heard
an oath pass his father's lips.   He had been
brought up to read his Bible, and to learn as
much of the meaning of it as his mother was
able to teach him.   Neither his father nor his
mother were able to do much more than read
and write.   They had not much education, and
were ignorant of a great deal that they would
have liked to know.   But they were devout and
simple-minded Christian folks, and had carefully
trained their little boy in all they knew themselves.   If Nat had something of the stern Puri-
tan element in his creed, Eileen on her part had
the vivid imagination and burning devotion of
her warm-hearted race, and Pat had inherited
much of her temperament, though not without
some of his father's hard-headed shrewdness.

Pat had begun to feel as though this lighthouse must be wonderfully near to God—much nearer than the crowded court where he had lived before. It seemed to him often as though God *must* be looking straight down out of heaven at the Lone Rock, and that there was nothing to come between Him and it, to hinder Him from seeing everything. So the child had got into the habit of thinking a great deal more than before of God; and it seemed very natural to think of Him to-night, with the great dome of star-spangled sky above, and the limitless black sea below, with the shining pathway across it that might be leading straight to heaven.

But Jim's words troubled him rather. He didn't like to think that Jim did not think about God too. He didn't see how he could help it in his long lonely night-watches. Pat knew very well that he should be frightened of the loneliness and the darkness if he wasn't quite quite sure that God would take care of him somehow, though how He did it the child was not at all certain. He went off on this train of thought now; and instead of answering Jim's remark, or asking him why he had not heard or thought about God for many years, he looked up into his face in a meditative fashion, and said, slowly and reflectively—

"I think He must send the angels to fly about the lighthouses at night and keep them safe. Mother says perhaps the stars are the angels' eyes looking down at us; and don't you think it feels like as if there were angels flying all about here? I think perhaps they like to dip their big beautiful white wings in the moon-light, like the sea-gulls. I almost think I can feel them flying round; it seems like as if there was a sound of wings in the air!"

"May be, little master, may be," answered Jim, without much interest in his face and tone. "If there be anything of that sort about the place, I make no doubt you would be the one to hear and see it."

Pat did not quite know what these muttered words might mean, nor could he get Jim to talk to him or sustain his share in the conversation. In point of fact, the talk grew very broken and disjointed, for the night air blowing on his face made the child very sleepy, and Jim was never one to speak by himself. How that night's adventure ended Pat never knew. He seemed soon to be flying all round the lighthouse on a pair of beautiful white wings, and trying to coax Jim, who stood on the gallery watching, to come and fly with him too. But Jim, though he had wings too, did not seem to have any wish to use them, and only stood still watching his companion, and refusing to trust himself to the flight to which Pat urged him, and the child was just trying to make him believe that it would all be right if he would only believe, when he felt a hand upon his head, and a voice said in his ear—

"Little son, little son, it is time you were waking, honey. The day has begun hours ago, and I can't find your clothes anywhere. Where did you put them when you took them off, Pat?"

Pat opened his eyes to find that he had no beautiful wings after all, and that he was just in his own bed, covered up very snug and warm, but when he threw off the bed clothes, there he found himself all dressed in those very clothes for which his mother had been hunting everywhere.

"Why, whatever does it mean?" cried Eileen, "the child has been walking in his sleep. Saints preserve us! but if he takes to that in this place it's never a wink of quiet sleep I will get!"

"Oh, mother, it was not in my sleep!" cried Pat, remembering all the adventure now. "I was wide awake. I wanted to see the big lamp alight, and I went up, and Jim let me sit with him, and he wrapped me up in his coat by-and-by, and took me out on to the gallery. And I suppose I must have gone to sleep there, and he must have brought me back to bed and wrapped me up like that. Mother, Jim is a very kind man. He isn't a bit like what I thought; I'm going to have him for a friend. I think by-and-by he will like me perhaps. I like him very much. He was very kind last night."

"Well, if anybody can come at his heart, it will be the child," thought Eileen, whose own advances had been steadily rejected and ignored. She was sorry for the lonely man with the sad history, and was a little afraid of him too; but when she whispered a word of her fear to her husband, Nat stoutly declared it was "all right." Pat could do as he liked, and make what advances he chose. The worst that could happen would be that Jim would turn a deaf ear to him. He would never harm the child. He was not that sort. There were stories against him, it was true ; but nothing they need fear as regards their own child. Nat was not troubled with a vivid imagination, and Eileen had long learnt to subdue her fears when her husband told her she was frightening herself about nothing. She would be glad enough to lighten the dreary lot of "Surly Jim," and watched with some curiosity the advances of Pat towards him.

At first little progress seemed made. At table the two hardly looked at each other, and Jim never spoke unless actually obliged ; but now and again she would see them sitting together in the boat, which had always been Jim's summer sitting-room, and gradually it seemed as though there was more talk between them. She could see that Pat began to chatter away freely enough, and sometimes she fancied that Jim took a share in the conversation. His pipe would go out, and be laid aside. He would lean towards the child, and seem to be listening with some intentness. Eileen was not a little curious to know what all this talk was about, but Pat was singularly reticent, and seldom spoke of Jim, though he would chatter to his mother about anything and everything else. Once she did venture to ask what they had been talking about, and got an answer that surprised her not a little.

"We talk about a lot of things ; Jim knows such a lot when you once get him to talk," said Pat, with a certain quiet reserve of manner. "But I think he likes it best when we talk about God. You see he'd almost forgotten about Him. He's remembering now, and it's very interesting. We've begun at the beginning of the Bible, and we skip a good deal, so we shall soon get to the part about Jesus, and I think that'll be the most interesting of all ! "

CHAPTER III

AN ODD PAIR

I T be queer to see them together. They be as thick as thieves," said Nat to his wife with a broad smile, as he sat down to table for the dish of tea he always looked for before he went up to see that all was in order with the lamp before the dusk fell. "As for me, I can't get a word out of him no how; but the little chap, he makes him talk as I never knew he could. I can't hear what they say. Bless you! if I so much as look that way, Jim shuts up his mouth like as if no power on earth would open it, and Pat he goes as red as a rose, as if he was half ashamed to be caught chattering; but so soon as my back's turned they're at it again. And glad I be that the poor chap has found somebody to love and to care for him; for he's had a hard life of it, if all we hear of him be true."

"That's just what I think, Nat," answered Eileen. "I'm glad the boy has found the way to his heart. Sure it's a bad thing for any creature to be shut up against his fellow-men as he was. May be it's the blessed saints as have sent the child to him to show him a better way."

Eileen still spoke sometimes about the "blessed saints," as she had been used to do in her childhood, when she lived amongst those who used even to pray to them; but her husband would smile and shake his head when he heard the words, and to-day he answered slowly and thoughtfully—

"Nay, my lass; it's no doing of the saints above—not that I'm one to say they are not blessed, nor that they may not look down upon us poor creatures here below and think of us as their brethren; but it's the Lord as rules the world for us, and gives each one of us a work to do for Him somehow; and if our boy has been sent as a messenger to this poor chap— as like enough he has—it's the Lord's own doing, that's what it is; and we won't say a

word to discourage him, not though it may
seem as though he'd got a tough job before him
if he's got to win back Jim."

The ready tears started to Eileen's eyes. She
came over and put her hand on Nat's broad
shoulder, bending to kiss him, though he was
not a man who as a rule cared to receive caresses
from even his own wife or child.

"It does me good to hear you talk like that.
Sure and it's the children who are often the Lord's
best messengers. I heard a holy man say once
as the beautiful angels were God's messengers,
and it does seem sometimes as though He used
the children too—may be because they are most
like the angels themselves—bless their innocent
little hearts!"

But Pat never thought about being an angel.
He only felt like a very happy little boy, whose
life had suddenly become exceedingly interesting, and who had so much to do every day that
the days never seemed quite long enough for all
he wanted to put into them. There was so
much to learn about the reef and the lighthouse,
about the big lamp and its bigger reflectors,
about the wonderful fog-horn which he had
as yet never heard at work, and about the

apparatus which kept all these wonders moving,
that his head fairly swam sometimes in the
effort to take in all that he saw.   He had one of
those inquiring minds which is not content just
to see what is done, but must know the why
and the wherefore of it all.   Nat was content to
know that certain results would follow certain
actions on his part, and he followed his instruc-
tions, with intelligence and diligence, but without fully comprehending the mechanism of which
he was the overseer.   Jim was the man who
more fully understood this.   He could put to
rights any small matter which had got out of
gear, without any appeal to the mainland.   He
had been so long on the Lone Rock that he was
familiar with every detail of the lighthouse
apparatus, and Pat would watch him with awe
as he climbed about the great lamp, and cleaned
the wheels and the levers with the air of one
who knew exactly what was the work of each.
And then he and the child knew the secret
about the creatures being alive, when everybody
else thought it merely a machine.   Jim always
spoke of it as " her," and Pat learned to do the
same, and to wonder sometimes why she never
awoke by day, but was always so quiet and still

when the sun was shining, though when the dusk fell upon the land she would wake up and shine, and go round and round with that strange monotonous noise he had learned to heed as little as the ceaseless plash of the waves. That secret knowledge shared by both made another link between the man and the child. And then, if Jim could only find words, he could answer Pat's questions about the working of the creature far better than the child's father could do. Pat grew greatly impressed by the depth and profundity of his knowledge, and came secretly to the conclusion that Jim was a marvel of learning and skill. He was greatly flattered that he was allowed to be on terms of such intimacy with him, and grew to think his gruff speech and silent habits a grace, and a sign of learning and wisdom.

It was with great satisfaction one day that Pat heard that he and Jim were to be left in charge of the lighthouse for a whole day, whilst his father and mother went ashore to lay in stores against the coming autumn and winter. The summer was waning now. Before very long the fierce equinoctial gales might be any time expected, and Nat was anxious to get

D

ashore before this present calm broke up, and thoroughly victual the rock against the winter. Eileen, too, had many things to think of, both for herself and the child, before the winter should set in. They had been in rather low water, owing to Pat's long illness, just before they came here, and had not any supply of warm clothing with them. Now that Nat had been drawing his pay all these months, there was plenty of money to purchase what was needed. Only she felt she must go ashore herself for the purpose; but she thought the expedition would be too fatiguing for the boy, and Pat was more than content to be left behind with Jim, to take care of the home and the lighthouse in his father's short absence.

It was a beautiful hot September morning when the boat put off from the rock, and Pat stood holding Jim's hand and waving his little cap to his parents, as Nat hoisted the sail to the light breeze, and the boat began to cut its way through the sparkling water in the direction of the shore.

"The top of the morning to ye!" shouted the child, who loved to air his little bits of Irish phrases when he was in high spirits. "Sure

it's a lovely day for a sail. Come back again
safe and sound, and we'll be waiting for you
here. Good-bye, mother dear. Take care of
yourself, mavourneen. It's meself as will be
thinking of you every hour of the day till the
boat brings you back safe again!"

The mother waved her hand, and Pat stood
looking till his eyes were too dazzled to see
clearly any longer, and then he drew Jim back
towards the house. His small face was full of
importance and gravity. He plainly felt himself
his father's deputy for the day, and the sense of
his position and the burden of his responsibilities
weighed upon him rather heavily.

"We shall have to watch her very carefully
all day, Jim," he remarked. "Because you see
she may know that father has gone, and try to
take advantage. We had a dog who used to do
that once. Mother always said he took advantage when father had gone off for the day. It
wouldn't do for things to go wrong before he
came back. You and I will have to be very
careful. Shall we go up and look how she seems
now?—and whether she is all asleep and quiet?"

Jim grinned in his queer way, but assented
at once.

"All right, little master, we'll go. I've got
to clean her up. But I think she'll be quiet
like all day. She's a wonderful one for sleeping
so long as the sun shines—that she is!"

"Yes, rather like a bat, isn't it, Jim? I read
a tale once in a book about a big bat with a
funny name. I think it was called a vampire.
I know it was very big indeed, and rather fierce.
Perhaps *she's* a kind of vampire; only you've
made her tame, and she doesn't hurt people
now. Did she ever hurt you, Jim? You don't
seem afraid of her a bit."

"Nay, she's never hurt I," answered Jim.
"She don't hurt them as know how to humour
her. She did break the arm of one man
once; but he was a rare fool and deserved what
he got. You've got to be a bit careful of her
when she's going; but if you mind her well she
won't hurt nobody."

They were mounting the stairs now, and Pat
seated himself to watch Jim at his mysterious
duties about the great She, as he had come
to call her in his own mind. He had seen
everything done a dozen times before; but
the interest and fascination was always new.
To-day he was permitted to help Jim a little

by holding his leathers and rubbers from time to time; and he felt that he should soon be able to climb about and clean himself, so familiar did he grow with all his companion's evolutions.

It took the best part of the morning to do all that was needed to make things ship-shape for night, and Pat presently went downstairs to get ready the simple mid-day meal his mother had prepared for them. He thought that it would be pleasant to eat it down on the rocks, for the tide was out, and as it was a spring tide there was more rock than usual uncovered. He carried everything carefully down, and presently Jim joined him, and they sat down together. Pat thought it was quite the nicest dinner he had ever tasted, down in the cool shadow of the rocks, with the waves washing up and down only a few feet away. He got Jim to light his pipe by-and-by, and to tell him some of his sailor stories (Jim, he noticed, always talked better when he was smoking), and after an hour had passed like that, Jim suggested to him that it was his turn to tell a tale.

Now Pat was very willing to take his turn, but he had not any big store of stories, and such as his mother had told him had all been related

to Jim before—all but the Bible stories, of
which, to be sure, there were plenty left to tell.
Pat sat nursing his knees and thinking. At
last he looked up into his companion's face
and asked reflectively—

"I don't think I've ever told you about Jesus,
have I? We've not got to Him yet in reading
out of the Book. But there's lots and lots
of stories about Him—real pretty ones, too. I
could tell you some of them, if you liked.
I don't think you know about Jesus yet; do
you, Jim?"

The man had slowly taken his pipe from his
lips whilst the child was speaking, and now sat
staring out over the sea with a look on his face
that somehow seemed new to Pat, and which
made him all of a sudden look different; the
little boy could not have said how or why.

"I used to hear tell of Him when I was
little," came the reply, very slowly spoken.
"My mother used to tell me of Him when I
was a little chap no bigger than you. But
I went off to sea when I couldn't have been
much bigger, and since then there's been nobody
to tell me of Him 'cept the gentleman in the
prison; and I didn't take friendly to what he

said, though I dare say he meant it all kind enough."

" Well, I'll tell you as well as I can," said Pat, settling himself to his task with some relish. " Perhaps you'll remember some of the things I forget, and mother could tell us it all afterwards, if we like. But I can remember a good lot—all the things that matter most. So I'll begin."

And Pat did begin, in rather a roundabout fashion, it is true, and with a good many repetitions and harkings back to things he had forgotten, but still with a zest and goodwill that atoned for many defects in style, and with the perfect faith in the truth of what he was saying, that gave a reality to the narrative which nothing else could have done. When it came to the story of the Crucifixion and the Garden of Gethsemane, Pat found, rather to his surprise, that the tears came into his eyes, and that once or twice he could hardly get on with the tale. He remembered that his mother had sometimes cried in telling it to him ; but he had never quite understood why. IIe began to feel as though he did understand now. When he was telling it himself to somebody who was listening,

like Jim, it all seemed so much more real.   He
wanted Jim to understand it all—just as his
mother wanted him to understand; and that
made him enter into the meaning of the story
as perhaps he had hardly ever done before.
He was glad when it came to the joyful part,
about how the Lord rose again, and showed
Himself to His doubting and mourning followers.
Jim never spoke the whole time, but sat with
his face turned out towards the sea, never
moving, and looking sometimes as though he
scarcely heard what the child said; yet Pat was
convinced that he was listening to every word.
It was only when the story had been finished
for several minutes that he slowly turned his
head round, and Pat saw with surprise that
there was a moisture in his eyes that looked
exactly as though it were tears.

"That's the story as my mother used to tell
it me," he said, in a husky voice.   "Do you
think as it's all true, little master?"

"Why, of course it's true!" answered Pat,
with perfect confidence.   "Almost everybody
in the world believes it—everybody except the
heathen!" (And Pat quite believed this was so.)
"Some folks forget, as you did, Jim, and some

don't care as they should. But it's every word
true. He did die."

" Yes, but why? Why did He die if
He needn't have done? Why did He let
them nail Him on the cross like that, if He
could have had as many angels as He liked
to come and take Him away out of their
hands?"

" Oh, because, you know, He came to die
for us," answered Pat, wrinkling up his fore-
head, and trying to remember how his mother
had answered *his* questions on this very point.
" He was the Lamb of God who came to take
away the sins of the world—your sins, Jim,
and mine, and everybody's. God could not
have forgiven everything if it hadn't been for
Jesus, because He is so just as well as so kind.
Somebody had to be punished—somebody had
to die for us. We couldn't have died for ourselves—not like that, you know, because we
are all wicked. It had to be somebody good—
like the lamb in the Passover, without blemish
—and that could only be Jesus. I don't know
if I can explain it right; but it's something like
that. There was nobody else, and God loved
us so, He sent His own Son. Oh, Jim, it *was*

good of Him! I don't think we love Him, or Jesus, half enough!"

Jim passed his horny hand over his eyes. He didn't speak for some time.

"It doesn't hardly seem as though He *could* have done it for us—for you and me," continued the child, filled with his own thought. "But He did, I know He did; mother says so, and it's all in the Bible, for she can find the places.

"I mean to try and think about it oftener, for it doesn't seem as though we ought ever to forget it. Mother says it ought to make us try and do things for Him; but I don't know what I can do, except to love Him, and try to be good. Perhaps till I'm bigger He'll let that count."

"And when you're bigger what will you do, little master?" asked Jim.

Pat sat and pondered the question a good while with his chin in his hand.

"I don't quite know," he answered slowly. "I mightn't ever have the chance; but I think I know what I should like to do if I could."

"And what is that?" asked Jim, with sudden and very evident interest.

"I think," answered the child, slowly and

reverently, " that I should like best to lay down
my life for somebody else—like as He laid it
down for us. Some people have done that,
you know—brave men who have died doing
their duty—to try and save other people from
death. I think God must love them for it.
I think Jesus must smile at them, for He did
just the same for us; and if He knows that
they do it because they want to be like Him
and do something for Him, I think He would
be pleased. People don't always die because
they are willing to; sometimes they are saved
too. But Jesus would know that they were
willing to die for Him. I think, when I grow
to be a man, if I might choose, I should like
best to serve Him like that."

Whilst Pat was speaking, Jim's eyes had
been fixed earnestly upon his face. Now they
roved back again over the sea, and suddenly
the man gave a great start. He rose to his
feet, and stood looking over the sea, shading
his eyes with his hand.

" What is it ? " asked Pat, coming and standing
beside him, and imitating his gesture. " Can you
see anything, Jim ? I can't seem to see nothing."

" That's just it," answered the man. " We

can't see half as far as we did an hour ago.
Seems like as if there was a thick sea-fog
coming on. I was thinking only this morning
what a time we had been without one. That's
a fog-bank and no mistake, and drifting right
down upon us, too. I must go and see to the
horn. We must start that if it comes over us;
else your father might never find his way back
—to say nothing of the ships running aground
here. You'll hear her voice, and no mistake,
little master, before another hour is over; and
a mighty queer voice it is, I can tell you.
You'll not forget it easy, once you've heard it!"

Pat was immensely interested. He followed
Jim up into the upper room, and went out upon
the gallery to watch the great fog-bank creep
slowly down upon them. The sun was so bright
and clear that it seemed impossible that that
slowly moving white mass should ever obscure
it; but soon a few little light vapour wreaths
drifted up against the rocks, and very quickly
the sun looked dull and red, and little by little
the sky and the sea seemed all to be blotted out,
and Pat could not tell which way he was looking,
nor where the land lay. He seemed to be up
alone in some high place, floating in mid-air,

in a world of vapour. He would have been frightened if he had not heard Jim moving about close at hand.

And then, all in a moment, a most fearful and extraordinary noise just above his head made Pat clap his hands to his ears, as though his head would come off with the vibration if he did not. He knew what it was. *She* had been awakened from sleep, and was lifting up that great voice of hers, as he had heard she could do when it was wanted; and in great amazement, Pat ran indoors to see how she did it. He felt that such a wonderful creature as this had surely never lived before!

CHAPTER IV

LONE ROCK IN FOG AND STORM

BUT strange and fascinating as was the voice of the great She, Pat could not be quite happy till his father and his mother had got back safe to the rock again. He could not imagine how they could find their way in all the thick wreaths of darkness which shut the Lone Rock in; but Jim told him that very likely it was quite clear a little way off, and that the noise of the horn, which sounded every three minutes, would guide his father safely to the right place. The sea was quite smooth and still; he could approach without any trouble. Jim knew that Nat would not be easy away from his post, more especially now that this fog had come on, which would entail extra care and extra work. There was a mechanical apparatus worked by steam, which could keep the horn blowing at intervals for a certain number of hours; but that required attention too, and for the present, Jim preferred to work it by the bellows, remaining up aloft, and bidding Pat keep watch for the boat below, if he liked, but to be very careful not to lose his footing on the rocks, as there would be nobody to come to his help.

Pat was not afraid of that now. He always ran about barefoot, and was as sure of foot as a goat by this time.

He stationed himself upon the great square rock overlooking the little creek where the boat usually lay moored, and watched the thick wreaths of vapour as they drifted and circled round him. Sometimes, for a few moments, they would clear away for a while, and he would be able to look out over the grey waters for some little distance. Then they would close over again, and shut out even the sight of the waves not ten feet below him, and Pat would feel as though he were quite, quite alone in a world of fog, with only the great horn overhead for company. But it was company, and kept him in mind that Jim was not far away, and so he was not frightened, although very

much surprised and perplexed by this strange
new experience.

It might have been an hour that he had been
watching, when he heard the plash of oars,
sounding a long way off, though in reality
they were quite close, and almost immediately
afterwards he saw the outline of the boat
looming large against the background of fog,
and uttered a joyful shout.

"Father! dear daddy! Mother, is that you?
I was so afraid you would never find your
way home; but Jim said you would. Did
you hear her blow the horn? Doesn't she do it
well? Isn't it nice that she can wake up when
she's wanted? She woke up and blew directly
Jim told her there was a fog. Isn't it queer
to be all thick like this? It isn't dark, but
we can't hardly see anything. Daddy, did
you ever see anything quite so funny before?
Mother, did you?"

"I've seen plenty of sea-fogs in my time,
my little son," answered Nat, as he brought
in the boat, and moored it safely in its niche;
"and I am always glad to see them go, for they
do more ill to ships, I take it, than storms
and tempests. I'm glad to find myself here;

for it's ill being at sea in such thickness as this. However, I think it will lighten a bit soon. The bank isn't a deep one, so far as I can see, and it must have pretty nigh drifted over us by now—not but what it may come back again a dozen times before the day is over. There is no telling what a fog will do. It's more capricious than a woman—eh, wifie?"

Eileen smiled as she stepped ashore. Her face was rather pale.

"I know more of women than of fogs, Nat. I don't know if they be much alike. Pat, darling, it's glad I am to see you safe and sound again. I'll not have to go ashore for a long while now. I've brought everything we shall want for many a month to come."

Almost as she spoke the fog began to lift, and in a few moments, to the astonishment of Pat, the sun was shining again quite brightly. A breeze sprang up and drove the floating vapours away, dispersing them hither and thither, and making the waves dance and foam round the rocks. The great horn ceased to make its doleful cry, and Jim came down from above to help to unload the boat.

"Have you got *my* parcel, mother?" asked

E

Pat, edging up to her, and speaking in a whisper, as thing after thing was brought in by the two busy men. The mother smiled and nodded, and presently she opened a big square package, and drew forth a small parcel tied up in brown paper, at sight of which Pat's face kindled all over.

"Is it a nice one, mother? And did you spend my bright half-crown?" And on being satisfied upon these points, Pat vanished with his treasure into an inner room, and proceeded to untie the string and carefully open the mysterious parcel.

When he had removed the two wrappings of paper, his eyes brightened and glowed with delight. He saw a beautiful book, with red-gold edges, in a soft black morocco cover, and he turned the leaves with reverent, loving fingers, and placed the book-mark in the place where he had been planning to read next to Jim—the place where the story of Jesus began that they had been talking over this very day.

"It's a prettier Bible than mine," thought the child; "but mother gave me mine, so, of course, I like it best, and I shall always keep it as long as I live. But Jim will like this, I know; and he hasn't got any Bible, though he says he can read, and used to like to read once. I'm sure he'll like it. I'll go up to-night and give it him when he has his watch. He can read it up there in the tower when he's not attending to her. There's plenty of light, and in the winter he says the nights do seem long. It'll be nice for him to read about Jesus, and all the stories that are in the Bible."

So as soon as supper was over, whilst his father and mother were still busy putting away the ample stores of provisions and clothing that they had brought from the mainland, Pat stole upstairs with his treasure in his hands, and came and took his favourite seat by Jim's side, still keeping the book safely hidden beneath his jacket.

" Jim, don't you never read of a night up here alone ? " he asked.

"I don't often now. I did use to read the paper a bit, whenever I get a few sent over from shore; but one gets out of the habit of it, and sometimes there's nothing to read for days and weeks together."

" I like reading," said Pat; "and I thought

you'd perhaps like it too if you had something interesting to read. I've brought you a book. Mother got it for me to-day. It's yours now, for I've written your name inside, so that nobody can't ever take it away from you; and I think it would be nice if you would read it sometimes in the night. I'm almost sure you'll like it, if once you begin." And with a red but happy face, Pat pulled out his treasure, and presented it shyly to Jim.

The man took it and looked at it, and then at the child, as though he didn't know what to make of so strange a thing as a present. Perhaps it was a dozen years since he had received a gift of any kind.

"Be it for me, little master?" he asked in a puzzled voice.

"Yes, to be sure it is," answered Pat, beaming. "I got mother to choose it for you, because she always chooses so well. It's a Bible, Jim. It's got all the stories in that we like to talk about, and all the story of Jesus—what we talked about to-day, and you liked. I've put the mark in one of the places where it begins about Him. You can read it yourself, if you like, whilst you're watching her."

It was so long since Jim had ever received such a thing as a present that he scarcely knew how to thank the child, but kept turning the book over and over in his hands with a sheepish look on his face. However, Pat was easily satisfied, and he knew that Jim was more pleased than he showed; so he slipped down the stairs again in a happy frame of mind, and found his father examining the weather-glass below—a mysterious object in the child's eyes, which he always regarded with awe.

" A good thing we went ashore to-day, wife," Pat heard his father say. " For if I don't mistake me, we'll have a spell of rough weather on us soon. The glass is going down steady and fast. By to-morrow morning, I take it, it'll be blowing half a gale of wind."

Pat looked wonderingly at the glass, and could not see that it had moved from its niche. He never could understand why his father would say that it was higher some days than it was on others ; but it was one of those things that he never asked about—one of those mysteries that he pondered over in secret with a sense of wonder and rather fascinating awe.

Next morning he was not awakened, as he

had been of late, by a bar of sunshine slanting
across his bed and touching his face. He awoke
later than his wont to a sound of moaning and
splashing which he had not heard before; and
when he jumped up and ran to the window
he saw that there were heavy banks of cloud
scudding across the sky, whilst the sea had
turned from blue to grey, and was dashing itself
against the rocks with greater vehemence than
he had ever seen before. There was a moaning
sound all around the walls of his home, rising
sometimes to a mournful shriek. The little
boy was glad to get on his clothes, and find a
glowing fire burning in the living room. There
had come a chilliness into the air, and it seemed
as if summer had suddenly taken flight. His
mother looked up at him as he came, and
greeted him with a smile.

"Well, Pat; so father is right after all, and
here are the gales come upon us all sudden-like
at the last. We shall have to make up our
minds to a deal of moaning and tossing and
tumbling if we are to live all the winter in a
lighthouse! You'll be a brave boy, my little
son, and not mind the wind and the rain and
the dashing of the waves? It'll not frighten

you to hear it day after day and week after week, will it, honey?"

"Frighten me?" asked Pat, almost indignantly. "Why, mother, no! I'm almost a man now, and men aren't frightened by noises. I shall help father and Jim to take care of the lighthouse, and I'll help you down here when I'm not too busy upstairs with her. Jim says there's a deal more to do in winter than in summer, and sometimes they'll be very glad of a third man to help. I shall be the third man here. I shall have lots to do and think about!" And Pat looked for all the world like an important little turkey-cock, and went running up the stairs to see what was going on there, whilst his mother looked after him with a smile, and breathed a thankful prayer to God for giving back her child such full measure of health and strength.

The next weeks were very interesting and exciting ones to Pat. The wind blew strongly and steadily, and the sea ran higher and higher. He used to go out daily into the balcony round the lamp-house, and stand "to le'ward," as Jim used to call it, whilst he watched the great crested waves come racing along, and breaking into sheets of spray at the foot of the reef—spray which sometimes rose almost as high as he was standing, and would often make the mackintosh coat in which he was always wrapped fairly run down with water.

Jim would stand beside him sometimes, and tell him how in winter storms the spray would dash not only as far as the gallery, but right over the top of the lighthouse. Pat found it hard to believe this at first, but as he came to learn more and more of the marvellous power of the sea, he disbelieved nothing; and used sometimes to say with awe to Jim, when he had finished one of his stories of shipwreck and peril—

"It do seem wonderful that the sea obeyed Jesus when He was here, and went down and got still just when He told it to. Mother says God holds the sea in the hollow of His hand. Jim, I think God's hand must be very wonderful; don't you?"

Perhaps nothing so helped those two to understand the mighty power of God as their lonely life in the lighthouse during those stormy autumn days. If any story in the Bible reading seemed too marvellous for belief, it only needed

Pat to point over the sea with his little hand,
and remark reflectively, "But you see, Jim, He
made all *that!*" to convince them both that
nothing was too hard for the Lord. The story
of Peter's attempt to walk on the sea was one
of their favourite readings, when once they had
come across it. Jim was wonderfully taken by
the tale, and would have the mark kept in the
place for a long time.

"I read it every night up here alone," he
said once to Pat, "and I can't help wondering
if I could ever walk on the sea if I asked Him
to help me."

"Perhaps He would if you were going to
Him," said Pat reflectively. "I don't know
if He would for anything else. You see, He'd
said 'Come' to Peter, and so he could do it,
until he got frightened and forgot the Lord
had called him. Mother says that was why
he began to sink—because he'd begun to think
about himself, instead of trusting it all to
Jesus. If he were to say 'Come' to you,
Jim, and you were to go out to meet Him, I
expect it would be all right. But He don't
seem to call folks in that sort of way now."

New experiences were becoming common

enough in Pat's life now, but he never forgot one curious sight which he was once called up from his bed to see in the middle of the night. He had gone to bed amid an unusual tumult of sound—moaning wind and dashing spray, and sometimes such a bang as a great wave struck the wall of the tower—that for some time he could scarcely get off to sleep, seasoned though he was to such sounds.

Then, in the middle of the night, he was awakened by Jim coming to fetch him, and when he was once fairly awake, he was delighted to hurry into his warm suit of weather-proof clothes, and follow Jim upstairs, for he thought that the time had surely come when the services of the third man were required, and very grand and important he felt to occupy that proud position.

But it was not quite what he thought, after all; for though his father was on watch as well as Jim whilst the storm raged round the lighthouse, there was nothing very much to be done, save to see that the light burned brightly, and Pat wondered for a moment why he had been summoned.

"Jim said you'd like to see the birds, sonny,"

said his father, taking him in his strong arms,
and holding him up near to the glass : " so I
said he could fetch you.   Look ! do you see
them flying against the glass ?   It's the light as
brings them these stormy nights.   They know
they'll get perching-room somewhere round, if
they get nothing else.   See their white wings
flitting to and fro, Pat ?   Jim says in the morning we shall pick up a score or so of dead birds
in the gallery, as have dashed their lives out
flying straight against the glass."

Pat looked and began to see, for at first his
eyes were dazzled.   It was just as his father
had said : outside the glass house were multi-
tudes of wild sea birds, flitting to and fro like
ghosts in the black darkness, and every now
and then dashing themselves against the strong
dome of glass with a noise which told of the
violence of the effort.   There seemed to the
child to be an endless myriad of white and
grey birds circling round his sea-girt home,
and he looked at them in wonder and awe, for
he had never before seen so strange a sight.

" Do they want to get in, father ? " he asked
softly.   " Oh, let us open the door and take
them in.   They are frightened at the storm.

Why should we not let them come in and warm themselves here?"

"They would only be worse scared than they are, Pat," answered his father, "and would fly into the lamp and hurt themselves and it. Poor foolish things! they don't know what they come for themselves; it's just the light attracts them. We'll get feathers enough to stuff a pillow for your mother to-morrow, if Jim is right about what we shall find outside."

But Pat was quite unhappy about the poor foolish wild birds driven seawards by the gale, and coming to the lighthouse, as it were, for shelter.

"Let me go outside and see them there," he said; and Jim wrapped him up warmly and carried him out for a few minutes.

It was a still stranger sight out there to see the strange antics of the bewildered birds, and to hear their cries and screams, which made Pat shiver in spite of himself, remembering the stories his mother sometimes told him on winter evenings of the "banshee" and its wailing cry. He was dreadfully sorry for the birds, but they would not let him come near them, and he saw that nothing could be done for them.

"I suppose God knows about them," he said at last, with a great sigh. "If He cares for sparrows, I suppose He cares for sea-gulls, too. If He knows, I suppose we need not mind very much. But I should have liked to take them in and feed them, and make them warm and comfortable. They sound so very sad; but perhaps God will comfort them best."

And then Jim carried the child down to his warm bed again, and he fell asleep, thinking of the birds and their strange noises and ways.

He awoke with the same strange noise in his ears. He was sure it was a voice like that of a sea-bird. He started up and looked about him, and then the sound came again. It was broad daylight now, and the noise seemed to proceed from the adjoining living room. Pat jumped up, and ran in without troubling to put on his clothes till his curiosity was satisfied.

"Mother, what is it? What is that queer noise?" he asked; and then he saw a basket standing in a corner of the room, and the noise seemed to proceed out of that.

"Go and get dressed, dear," answered his mother, "and then Jim, may be, will be down again. It's a wild bird that has hurt itself

that he's got there. He thought you might
like to have it to take care of till it got well,
but it's so wild and fierce, and bites so, that I
daren't open the basket till he comes. Jim
says they fly at folks' eyes sometimes; but he
seems to know how to manage it. Get you
dressed, honey, and then he'll show it you."

Pat was not long dressing that morning, and
as soon as Jim could be got down from the
tower, the basket was opened, and the treasure
inside displayed to the child's admiring eyes.
It was a young gull, whose wing was badly
broken—so badly, that Jim declared it would
never fly again, and was of opinion that the
most merciful thing to do would be to pinion
it—since it was the end of the wing that was
broken—and bring it up to be a tame bird
upon the rock, living there and catching fish
in the pool, but kept from swimming away
altogether by a light fetter round its foot. He
had kept birds on the rock before now that had
hurt themselves against the glass, though when
they had grown quite strong and well they had
usually taken themselves off. Still, he had
sometimes kept pets for some considerable
time; and Pat was all on fire to tame this

gull, and make a playmate of it. It was not
a very promising playmate at first, for it was
wild and fierce, almost past management, and
Pat thought it would have died under Jim's
hands when he performed with skill and
rapidity the operation which was soon seen
to be a wonderful relief to the suffering
bird. It refused food for two days, and the
child feared it would certainly die; but his
patience and care were unwearied, and at last,
on the third day, it began to feed from his
hand, being too weak to fear him; and after a
few mouthfuls of fish greedily swallowed, it
rewarded its friend by a vigorous peck on the
hand, which nearly drew blood. Pat, however,
was not at all discouraged, but looked upon it
as a sign of returning health; and by slow
degrees, as the days and weeks wore away, a
certain confidence and friendship grew up between the wild bird and the little boy who
tended him so faithfully and regularly.

Jim contrived a little aviary for the bird—
if so grand a word could be applied to the wire
erection down among the rocks, where the bird
could get salt-baths at high water, and fish in
the pools left by the retiring tide—by the side

of which Pat spent hours every day teaching
the gull to come and take food from his hands,
and gradually establishing a freemasonry between them, which developed at last into a
real friendship, so that the little boy could go
fearlessly into the cage at the wider and taller
end against the house, and call the gull to perch
upon his knee, and take bits of fish even from
between his lips, and take any liberties he
chose with his captive without fear of a rebuff.

This new pastime was a source of immense
pleasure to the little boy through the long
dreary days of winter. He never felt dull in
his strange home; and with Jim to talk to,
the lamp to watch, and his bird to teach
and tame, the days flew by all too fast, and
he could scarcely believe when Christmas was
actually upon them.

It was a queer Christmas, spent amongst
the sounds and sights of the Lone Rock, with
the wild waves lashing the walls of his home,
and the moaning of the wind for the only
music. But Pat was growing used to the life,
and did not call it queer now. It seemed far
stranger to think of going back to the crowded
court, where they never saw or heard the sea,

"At last, on the third day, it began to feed from his hand."—*Page* 79.

F

and where even the sky and the air seemed quite different.

But it was interesting to explain to Jim about Christmas Day being Jesus's birthday; and the child discovered to his great satisfaction and surprise that it was Jim's own birthday, too. He had been born on Christmas Day, just as Pat had been born on Patrick's Day, to the great satisfaction of his Irish mother; and so the festival of Christmas was kept as brightly as it was possible, and neither Nat nor his wife could fail to remark how changed in many ways Jim was from what he had been in the spring, when first they had come to the rock.

"I believe it's the love of the Lord coming into his heart that's doing it," said Nat, as he sat over the fire with his Bible, when Pat had gone to bed, and Jim was up aloft. "He took first to the child, and the child has led him to the Lord. It's often the way with us poor frail human creatures. We seem as though we must have some human hand to lead us, though the Lord is holding out His wounded hand all the while, and bidding us take that. It's wonderful true those words of His about the babes and sucklings. It seems to me that the heart of a little child is coming in place of the hard heart Jim seemed to have before. May be the Lord has a work for him to do yet. It may be we were sent here partly for him. One never knows where the work will meet one in the vineyard; but we must try to be ready for it when it comes."

CHAPTER V

LTHOUGH there had been plenty of wind, and a heavy sea running for the greater part of the winter, Pat had not seen what Jim called a "real storm" until Christmas had been several weeks old, and January had nearly run its course. The child called any rough bout of windy weather a storm, and did not quite believe that Jim could be right in declaring that it was "only a capful of wind," or that it was "only half a gale, after all." But there came one night late on in January when he began to understand very well what Jim had meant, and to realise that he had not really understood before what a real winter storm could be like.

All day there had been a strange new sound in the moaning and the shrieking of the wind.

His father had looked often at the glass, and had remarked almost every time he did so that "they were going to get it this time, and no mistake." Jim had been so busy up aloft that Pat had hardly seen him since breakfast-time; and even the sea-gull seemed to partake in the general uneasiness, for he flapped his wings, and screamed and cried in a way that was quite unusual for him; and when Jim came downstairs about dinner-time, he walked out to the side of the cage where the child stood watching his favourite, and said—

"I'd bring him indoors to-night, Pat. I'd not answer for it but that the water will be over here before morning. Anyway, there's be sheets of spray flying about enough to drown the bird, if he's left where he is."

Pat looked up wonderingly, for though one end of the great caged-in place ran down towards the lower rocks, the upper end was against the lighthouse itself, and it seemed impossible to the child that the waves should ever reach as high as that. He had lived seven or eight months in his new home by this time, and had never seen the sea as high as that yet. But of course Jim must know best.

"I'll bring him in," he answered readily. "Mother won't mind if you tell me to, and he does come in sometimes. He hardly ever pecks at anybody now. See how tame he is when I go to take him!"

Pat was rather proud of the conquest he had made of the bird, and certainly the wild creature made no resistance to being lifted by his little master and carried within doors. Eileen looked up as Pat brought the captive in with him.

"Poor thing! so he wants shelter to-night, does he! Put him there in that bit of a cupboard, Pat dear, with a wire netting in front of him to keep him from cluttering up my clean kitchen. There, he can see you now, and you can see him. What a pretty bird he's growing! I'm sure he's welcome to a place within doors. God help all those poor souls who will be out at sea to-night!"

The woman spoke with so much earnestness and feeling, that Pat looked up in her face with wide-open, questioning eyes.

"What makes you say that, mother? Is it going to be what Jim would call a real big storm? I rather wanted to see one. Is it

naughty to feel so? I won't, if it is; but I
thought a lighthouse boy ought to know what
a real storm was like. Are we going to have
one to-night, mother?"

"I fear we are, my child. And terrible it
will be for those who are afloat, exposed to the
mercy of the wind and the waves. We must
pray to God for them, my little son; for in
times like these only God can help them, and
perhaps there are some in peril to-night, who
will never pray for themselves—though in the
hour of danger it is wonderful how the human
heart turns to the God of heaven, however
hard at any other time."

Pat's eyes were open wide, and a new look
had crept into them.

"Mother, shall we pray now?—you and I
together?" he asked; and Eileen took his
little hand in hers, and knelt down then and
there on the kitchen floor, praying aloud in
very simple words for those in peril on the deep
that night, that God would be with them in
every danger, and bring them safe at last to
the haven whither they would be. And Pat
shut his eyes tight, and clasped his hands, and
said "Amen" softly, several times, adding, as

his mother ceased, "And if there are any little boys like me, please keep them quite safe, dear Lord Jesus, and bring them safe back to their mothers again."

And then, when the child opened his eyes, and rose from his knees, he saw that Jim had crept in, all unknown to them, and that he was kneeling, too, his head down-bent, and a tear slowly trickling down his weather-beaten face. Pat had never seen him on his knees before. He had never been able to get Jim to tell him whether he ever said his prayers at all. But he was sure now that he did, and he ran across to him before he had had time to rise to his feet, and throwing his arms about his neck, he cried out—

"Now we have all prayed to God together, so I'm *sure* He'll hear us. He likes there to be two or three gathered together—it says so, somewhere in the Bible. I shan't be so unhappy about the poor people in the ships now, because we've asked God to take care of them, and He always hears what we say— doesn't He, mother?"

"Yes, dear, He always hears," answered Eileen, with a smile and a sigh. "But He does not always answer us quite in the way we would have."

"But, then, He knows best," said Pat, with sudden thoughtfulness. "So if He does it differently from what we meant, we needn't mind, need we? You don't always do just what I want, mother dear; but afterwards I always know you decided best. It's like that with God and us, I suppose."

Eileen stooped with a tear in her eye to kiss the child, and Jim went out to help Nat to haul up the boat, and place it in the greatest security the rock offered, to leeward of the wind, well braced at both ends to keep it steady. Pat watched these operations with great interest.

"But why do you take it out of the water?" he asked. "I should have thought you's want it there in case any ship in distress should go by. You might want to send a boat out to them, and if it was up here you wouldn't be able to get it out at all quickly."

"No boat could live in such a sea as we'll have to-night, sonny," answered the father gravely. "Nothing but a life-boat, anyhow, and then it could not be launched here amongst these rocks. Look at those waves, now. Do you think there would be any putting out to sea amongst such rollers as those? No, my little son. Please God we'll keep our light burning brightly—which is the duty given us to do—and that will help the big ships to keep clear of this cruel reef, where the best of them would be dashed to pieces. But more than that we cannot do, and may God grant that no vessel comes nigh these rocks to-night. None will, unless she be disabled; but, if she did, we could do almost nothing to help her. God alone could direct her course that she should not be dashed in pieces on this treacherous coast."

So Pat went indoors, looking very grave, and feeling sobered by the shadow of peril resting upon some lives; and already the dark lowering clouds seemed to be driving faster and faster along the sky, and the shrieking of the wind grew ever angrier and angrier as the daylight waned.

Bang! bang! bang! It was only the waves flinging themselves in wild fury against the rocks upon which the lighthouse was built, but Pat felt the tower shudder beneath the shock, and looked into his mother's face as though to ask if they themselves were in any danger. Her face was grave and a little pale, but there was no personal fear in her steady eyes as she met the child's look, and answered it by a thoughtful smile.

"The walls of our home have stood through many a winter's storm, Pat. It's not ourselves we need fear for to-night, but for those at sea, in disabled vessels; and I fear me there will be many such upon a night like this. Hark at the wind! It is rising every moment!"

It was indeed, and Pat soon became too excited to do anything but wander up and down the stairs, watching the wild strife of the wind and waves, first from one place and then from another, not knowing whence the best view was obtained. He might not open the door upon the gallery to go out there, as he would have liked. Jim told him he would not be able to stand there in such a night; and that the air rushing and sweeping in would be bad for the lamp; and to-night, above all nights, she must be studied and thought of. Many, many lives might depend upon her light, and she was the object of the most scrupulous care on the part of both the men in charge of her.

"It seems as if she was trying to shine as bright as possible," said the child, with fond pride, as he looked up into the great ball of white flame above him. "Do you think she knows that there is a storm to-night, Jim, and is trying to throw the light as far as ever it will go?"

"I shouldn't wonder," answered Jim. "Her knows a power of things by this time, her does;" but he spoke absently, as though his thoughts were far away, and he kept moving across to one of the small windows which looked out over the wild tossing sea, as though to make sure that there was no indication of the presence of any vessel in distress on the horizon. Pat grew nervous at the silence of the man, and the furious noises of the raging storm without, and crept downstairs to his mother again.

By this time it was getting very dark. The tide was rising—a high spring tide—and the waves seemed to come thundering against the very walls of the lighthouse itself, making them shake to their foundations. Pat often looked

anxiously into his father's face to know what
he thought about it; but he knew the tower
was safe, and was only thinking of the perils of
others, like his wife.

"It is going to be a fearful night," he said,
as he rose from the tea-table. "There will be
no sleep for either of us to-night, wife. We
must both watch whilst the gale blows like
this. I'll send Jim down now to get a bite
and sup, and then he can join me up aloft.
You and the child can go to bed when you
will. Only leave us a good fire here, and something hot to take if we get chilled and wet."

"I shall not go to bed, Nat," answered
Eileen. "I could not sleep, and I shall keep
my vigil for those poor souls who are in deadly
peril to-night. There be times when it seems
heartless to lie down and sleep. If we were
in fearful danger ourselves, we should like to
know that there were those ashore praying for
us, even though they knew not our names."

Nat kissed his wife and child, and his
weather-beaten face looked tender.

"Well, well, my lass, please yourself, please
yourself. It will make the fireside brighter for
a man to come to if you are there to-night."

"Mother," said Pat, coming up and laying a small hand on her knee, "may I stay with you? May I keep a vigil, too? I know I could not sleep in my bed with all this noise of wind and waves. Please let me stop up too."

"Very well, my child; until you grow sleepy you may. We will watch together, and be ready to help the men, if help is needed. In such a storm as this one never knows what will befall. We will be ready whatever betide."

Jim came down to his tea next, and Pat eagerly asked him whether he had ever known such a storm before. He was surprised that Jim was not more filled with wonder at it than he was; but supposed that he had grown used to such tempests, as indeed was the case, for no winter ever went by without some such storm as the present one.

When mother and child were together again, Pat occupied himself for a while in feeding and playing with his bird, who was a good deal disturbed by his new surroundings, but was content to be coaxed and quieted by his little master's hand and voice. By-and-by

he retired to the back of the cupboard where
it was dark, and seemed to settle himself down
for sleep. By this time the tea-things had
been washed up, and the room made bright
and tidy. There was little more to do that
night, save to see that there was food and
something hot for the watchers at intervals,
when they should be able to come down for
it; and at Pat's suggestion his mother got
out her needlework, whilst Pat brought out
the big Bible from which his father generally
read a chapter aloud every day, and laying it
on the table, drew his high chair up to it, and
began turning over the leaves to find all the
places where it told of the sea, and especially
of any storms; which passages he then read
aloud to his mother, and they discussed them
afterwards together to the sound of the stormy
voices from without, which made a fitting
accompaniment.

As the night wore on the gale seemed rather
to rise than fall. There were times when the
child's voice could not be heard for the wild
shrieking of the wind without. Now and
again Pat would creep up the stairs to the
lamp house, and report to his mother, with an

awed face, that the spray was dashing right over the top of the tower. Sometimes one or other of the men would come down to sit awhile by the fire, and refresh himself with the good cheer Eileen had ready. Now and again Pat would dose off into a little light sleep, leaning against his mother's knee. But he would not hear of going to bed, and, indeed, there was no chance of continuous sleep, even for those used to the sounds of the winds and waters; for it was one continual battle without of raging strife, and Pat never slept long without waking up with a start at some crash of water against the wall, or some wilder shriek of the furious gale sweeping round the tower.

But, hitherto, there had been no sight or sound of human peril or distress. Each time that a watcher had come down, Eileen had anxiously asked if he had seen any vessel in peril, or had heard any signals of distress, and each time the answer had been that nothing of the kind had been seen or heard. Eileen breathed a sigh of thankfulness each time the report was made, and as the night wore away, and the storm did not seem to be increasing, she began to try and coax Pat to be put to

G

bed, for he was growing very sleepy at last, and had kept his vigil very bravely and well.

Her persuasion seemed just about to triumph over the child's reluctance to own himself sleepy, when a new sound suddenly smote upon their ears, causing Eileen's hand suddenly to fall to her side, whilst her face put on a look of white dismay and terror. For a moment she stood as rigidly as though she had been turned into stone, and Pat woke up wide in his surprise, for he had not understood the sound he had heard, and could not account for the change which had come over his mother. And then he heard again the faint new sound—only a distant report—the sound as of a gun.

"What is it, mother?" he asked in his perplexity.

"God help them—that is the signal gun. That is a ship in distress! There it is again! Oh, dear Lord Jesus, be with those poor souls in their hour of peril, 'for vain is the help of man!'"

Pat was wide awake now. His heart was beating fast and hard. Something of his mother's awe had communicated itself to him;

but inaction was not possible in this time of excitement. He must be doing something, and without another word or question he darted up the stairs to go and find his father and Jim, and ask them what they knew about this ship in distress.

They were both at a look-out hole. His father had the telescope, and Jim was shading his eyes with his hand, and gazing out into the night too intently to be aware of the presence of the child. The moon was full, and in spite of the wrack of clouds in the sky, the night was not wholly dark, and from time to time a shaft of light would stream out upon one portion of the sea or another, showing to the watchers something of the dismasted vessel beating helplessly in the trough of the raging sea.

"'The Lord help her, for she cannot help herself!" exclaimed Nat, as he handed the glass to Jim. "She's a fine vessel—a steamer; but her fires are out—may be her screw is broken—and the mast is snapped clean in half. It may be they will reach the lee of yon promontory before they are beaten to pieces. That is what they are making for plainly, and the vessel is well handled. But what can any helmsman do with such a crippled log? There is another gun! Would God we could help them, poor souls. But there is nothing we can do, and she is a good mile from the rocks, thank Heaven! If she can but weather it out for another half-hour, and keep the course she is making, she may get in safely yet. Or the lifeboat may see her, and take her passengers ashore. But 'tis a fearful thing to see her labouring like that in such a sea. Every wave seems as though it would swallow her up!"

"Daddy, let me see," pleaded Pat, and Jim adjusted the telescope so that the child could see the great disabled vessel lying rolling helplessly in the trough of the angry water, driven along almost at the mercy of the winds and waves, yet gallantly striving to keep such a course as should give her her only chance of safety. Pat was not seaman enough to estimate her chances of escape, and cried out every moment that she must sink.

Jim was afraid rather she would be driven in and dashed upon the rocks; but that she was under able management both men saw; and when Nat carried the child down to his mother, and saw Eileen's white face and straining eyes, he was able to kiss her, and place the boy in her arms, saying, "Please God, they will weather it yet; but 'tis a fearful thing to see. They have escaped being driven on this reef; and if they can get round the next point, they may find shelter from the gale. Pray for them, my lass, for it is all we may do. We will watch while you pray, and may be they will be safe yet!"

CHAPTER VI

JIM'S EXPLOIT

I'T'S a little boy! It's a little boy! Daddy! Oh, mother, look! look! I see him quite plain! It's a little boy. Oh, save him! save him!"

Pat's shrill little voice, sharpened by fear and pity, rang high through the noise of wind and waves. The cold dawn was breaking over the Lone Rock, and its four inmates were standing together at the base of the lighthouse with their eyes eagerly fixed upon the vast sheet of heaving and tossing water. The wind had abated its fury somewhat during the past hours, but the sea was still raging like a wild thing round the sunken reef. The tide, however, had fallen, and there was safe foothold for the little group anxiously gathered together. For some minutes

they had all been gazing in the same direction
—had been looking towards an object floating
in the water, drifting nearer and nearer to them ;
and now the child's shrill cry broke the silence,
and spoke the words the men had not dared
to do, though for some moments they, too, had
known what it was, lashed to a floating spar,
that was being drifted down upon the Lone
Rock.

" It's a little boy !   It's a little boy ! " cried
Pat, in an agony of sorrow and fear.   " Oh,
father !   Oh, Jim !   Will he be killed ?   Will
he be killed ?   Oh, don't let him be killed !
Don't let the waves dash him on the rocks !
Oh, what can we do ?   What can we do ? "

Eileen covered her eyes with her hand as
though to shut out the sight of the thing that
seemed as though it must happen.   It would
be too frightful to see that little frame dashed
in pieces before their eyes, even though life
might be already extinct.   Pat was clinging to
her dress in an agony.   Nat's voice shook as he
made reply to his child—

" I'm afraid he's dead already, Pat.   He may
have been hours in the water with the waves
dashing over him.   The life is soon beaten out

of a strong man like that. A little child could scarce live half-an-hour."

"Oh, save him! save him!" cried the child, his voice rising almost to a shriek. "Oh, I don't believe he's dead! See, his head is quite out of the water—only when the waves wash over it. I don't believe he's dead. Oh, don't let him be killed! Save him! save him!"

Nat shook his head sadly. He gave an expressive glance at his wife, and she gathered her own child in her arms and sank upon her knees, weeping and mingling prayers and supplications with her tears. Nat stood perfectly still and rigid, his gaze fixed upon the spar which carried the body of the child—whether living or dead none could tell—towards those cruel rocks which (if dashed upon them) would surely tear it in pieces before their very eyes. It was a moment that none of those ever forgot who had taken part in it. And only some minutes later did they observe that Jim had moved, and was no longer with them.

Pat was the first to note this. He raised his white, tear-stained face from his mother's shoulder, and looking round quickly, asked

with sudden eagerness, as though some new idea
had struck him—

" Where is Jim ? "

That made them all look round, and then
they all saw that Jim had gone within doors,
and that he was now issuing forth with a life-
belt round him, to which was attached a long
coil of strong rope. He had taken off his coat,
his boots, and leggings, and had nothing on
but his shirt and trousers, which last was rolled
up to the knee. He looked a very strong, mus-
cular fellow as he stood rolling up his shirt
sleeves, his face set in lines of the most dogged
and resolute determination. Pat gave a little
shriek, and rushed forward towards him.

" Jim ! Jim ! what are you going to do ? "

Nat and Eileen had also come forward, and
Nat laid his hand on his assistant's shoulder—

" Thou art a brave fellow, Jim," he said (when
Nat was moved in spirit he had a way of resort-
ing to thee and thou which he had heard as
a child from his Quaker mother), " but thou
must not throw away thy life. It is certain
death to try and live in yon sea, and thou hast
thy duties here to think of. Thou must think
of that, too, my good comrade."

"I have thought of it," said Jim, "but yet I must go. I know what I am doing. Yon spar will not be washed upon the reef; it will be carried just beyond round the point where we stand. I shall spring off yonder into deep water as it is swept by and seize it, and you will pull me in—for with that burden in my arms I cannot swim. I have not lived all the years on Lone Rock not to know what may and may not be done. It will not be certain death——" He stopped suddenly short. He could not say that it might not be death, and already he had spoken more freely than he had been known to do to any one but the child.

Pat rushed up to Jim, and flung his arms round his knees. His face was all in a glow of loving admiration and enthusiasm.

"Jim! Jim! Are you going to save the little boy? Oh, Jim, can you bring him safe home to us? Oh, Jim, how brave and good you are! Oh, how I do love you! If I were a man I would go with you, I would, indeed!"

Then Jim did a very strange thing—strange at least for him—for he lifted the child up in his arms and kissed him; and Jim had never kissed Pat in his life before. When he held

Pat thus he could speak in his ear words that nobody could hear except the two themselves.

"Pat," he said, and his voice was rather husky, "it seems just as though the Lord Jesus had told me to trust myself to the waves—to come out to Him, in a manner of speaking, and not to be afraid of the boisterous waves or the wind. I don't expect to be able to walk on the water; but it seems like as though He would be there to help me. I've been wanting to find something to do for Him all these weeks. It seems like as though He said to me just now, 'Go and do that, Jim. It's one of My lambs that is in peril.' So I'm going. And if I don't come back alive, don't you fret, little master. It's all right. You know what you said yourself you would like to do if you had the chance when you were a man—just to lay down your life—as He did."

Pat's tears were running down his cheeks, but he could not try to stay Jim after that, though he realised then that the peril of the rescue would be great. The man put him gently down, and pushed him towards his mother, who took him within her sheltering arms; and then he made his way with Nat

cautiously to the very edge of the rocks towards the edge of that great basin—to leeward as it chanced to-night—of the lighthouse,
where the water was comparatively calm for
a few yards, and where if he sprang in he
would find depth to swim without being immediately caught up and hurled backwards by
the fury of the sea.

Nat saw that his strong and skilled comrade
had just a chance of doing what he meditated,
and yet escaping with his own life, and he
would not seek to hold him back. Every seaman, at one time, or another, risks his life for
his fellow-men, and Nat had not been backward
in deeds of bravery in his own time. But as
keeper of the lighthouse now, and with a wife
and child to think for, he could not have taken
his life in his hand to-night as Jim purposed to
do. Still, he could aid and assist his comrade
by his skill and strength, and judicious management of the rope ; and he knew that Jim's life,
when once he should have taken the plunge,
would depend entirely upon the strength and
foresight and management which he should
show. He beckoned his wife to his side, for she
was a strong woman, and had grown up amongst

scenes of this sort. Eileen understood him in a moment, and came and stood beside him with her hand upon the ropes, ready to second his every effort, and do her share in the work of rescue. Pat stood beside his mother, his little face calm and quiet now, his eyes fixed full upon Jim. There was something in the expression upon all those faces that a painter would have loved to transfer to canvas—a look of lofty courage, of self-renunciation and purpose. Not a word more was spoken ; the time for action had come, and all were nerving themselves for it.

Although all this takes time to tell, only a few minutes had passed since Pat's first cry before they were all standing here at the edge of the basin, where the boat in the summer months rode at anchor. The sea was sweeping wildly past just outside this small basin, and the great waves were bringing nearer with every heave the floating spar, upon which all eyes were bent. Even Pat now understood exactly what Jim meant to do. It would have been madness for him to try and stem the force of the waves—to attempt to swim out against them. But he might launch himself into the boiling sea, and swim with them just as they were carrying their burden past the lighthouse, and then if he could once grasp it, the united strength of those upon the rocks might be sufficient to haul the double burden back to shore. Nat had already made fast the end of the rope to a great pinnacle of rock, which rose up like a gigantic needle at the edge of the basin. But all knew that ropes had been known to break beneath the strain which would come upon this one, that the strands might be cut where it was tied to the rock; and there was just the possibility that those on shore might be pulled into the boiling gulf before Jim and his burden could be dragged ashore. Nat realised this possibility, and his face was very set and grave; for he had the lighthouse to think for as well as his wife and child; and he knew that many, many lives might depend upon that sleepless light. The keeper of the lamp must not desert his post, come what might. It would be a fearfully hard choice if it had to be made; but Nat did his duty. If it came to be a question between Jim's life and that of his own duty, Jim must go. To let himself be dragged into the vortex would not save the life of his comrade, but it

might cost the lives of tens and even hundreds
of fellow-men. Nat's face was set and stern as
all this flashed through his mind, but his reso-
lution did not waver.

"It's coming! it's coming!" cried Pat,
breaking the strained silence with a sudden
cry, and he pointed with his little hand towards
the dark fleeting mass on the water, which was
very near to them now. In the grey, but
steadily increasing, daylight they could see the
face of the little child—the damp hair floating
round it, the expression calm and tranquil, as
though the little one was sleeping in his
mother's arms. They could see, too, that there
was a great life-buoy about the child, so that
it's head had been kept well above the water.
It was just possible that life might be restored.
Sailors have wonderful experiences of such
returns to life after long immersion in the
water. Pat could not believe the little boy
was dead, and with breathless eagerness he
watched Jim quietly slip into the water, and
strike out in strong vigorous strokes for the
floating spar. Eileen put her hands before her
eyes for one moment at the plunge, and then
stood up calm and strong.

"God help him! God be with him!" she murmured softly under her breath, and Nat said "Amen" in deep steady tones.

"Wife," he said, after a moment's pause, "remember that the lighthouse is now thy charge and mine. That must be our first duty. We two are its keepers now. God grant we have not to choose between it and yon brave fellow; but if it be His will that it be so, we must remember our duty to those who placed us here, and to those who sail on the sea, and look to be guided by yon light."

She understood him in a moment, and nipped his hand.

"Pray God it come not to that," she said. "We are both very strong."

And then they held their breath to watch the bold swimmer, who was already beyond the shelter of the rocks, exposed to the full play of the sweeping billows, rising and falling like a cork on the face of the mighty deep, but with every strong stroke approaching more near to the object he had started to seek.

Nat was paying out the rope with a look of strained anxiety on his face. Suppose it should not prove long enough! Coil after coil was

payed out, and still Jim had not quite come
up with the floating spar. Would there be
enough? Heaven send he reach it soon!

A shout from the child. Pat had clambered
a little way above them to get a better view.
Now came a wild hurrah.

"He's got him! He's got him! Oh, brave
Jim! Strong Jim! Daddy, he's got him.
He's seized him fast. Pull him in! Pull him
in quick! Oh, his head keeps going under!
He can't help himself now! He keeps his
arms fast round the little boy. He's doing
something; I can't quite see what! Oh, I see
now . . . He's cut the rope that ties him to
the spar! I can see it floating away by itself.
But he's got the little boy! He's got him fast!
Oh, daddy, be quick! be quick! Don't let
Jim drown! His head does go under so
often! Make haste and pull him out! Oh, do
make haste! The waves are so big and fierce,
and wash over them so often. He always keeps
the little boy top; but he keeps going under
himself so much. Oh, dear, brave Jim! How
I do love you. Oh, daddy, that wave! There
was something floating just under the water.
It hit Jim; I'm sure it did! Oh, I hope it did

not hurt him! He keeps fast hold of the little
boy. Oh, they are coming nearer! Do make
haste! Do make haste! Oh, I hope they will
not both be dead! Oh, hold on strong, Jim!
Daddy will pull you in soon; but the sea is so
strong! Oh, how I wish the sea was not so
cruel! I know now why mother said that it
would be a blessed thing when there was no
more sea!"

Pat was too excited not to keep talking all
the time, though some of his words were piped
out in shrill tones to his parents below, and
some were said beneath his breath to himself.
Below at the edge of the basin Nat and Eileen
were straining over their task, pulling in the
rope hand over hand, and using the pinnacle of
rock as a lever to assist their efforts, their faces
set and pale, their muscles tense and quivering; for it was a hard task—harder almost than
their strength was equal to; for the rush of the
hungry water dragging their prey away was
very great, and they dared not relax their
efforts for one moment.

But Eileen's muscles seemed to be turned
into steel, and as Nat said afterwards, he could
scarce believe it was not a strong man who

stood at his side. The mother instinct in her made her fight as if for life itself for that unknown woman's child, whose life lay in the balance, as well as for honest Jim, who had served her husband so faithfully all these months, and had been such a friend to her own boy, too.

" We shall do it yet, wife—thank the Lord ! " spoke Nat at length, in laboured gasps, as the strain upon the rope grew less. When once they had drawn the lifeless burden out of the track of the sweeping waves, and into the comparative tranquillity of the little bay, their task was comparatively easy. Hand over hand the rope came in, bearing the strain well, and showing no sign of rupture, until at last Nat leaned over the edge of the basin, and grasped the child by his floating hair.

Not the least difficult part of the business now was the raising of the half-drowned pair— the rescuer and the rescued inextricably locked together—out of the water and on to the safe shelter of the rocks above. Jim was by this time as insensible as the boy he had risked his life to draw ashore, though Nat was confident that he still lived, as he had not been long enough in the water to be past restoring. But his bear-like embrace of the child was hard to undo; and only when the pair lay side by side upon the rocks did Nat's strong hands succeed in loosing that rigid clasp.

The moment the child was free, Eileen took the dripping form in her arms and bore it indoors. She scarcely dared to hope that the little fellow could be living. There was no means of knowing how long he had been in the water, but it must have been a long while. However, she laid him on her table, with a small cushion beneath his head, dried and chafed his cold limbs, and applied a steady and gentle friction in the neighbourhood of the heart. Presently she was almost certain she detected a faint pulsation, and redoubled her efforts, disregarding Pat's entreaties that she would bring the little boy to the fire because he must be so cold.

"Wait a bit, honey," she answered, still rubbing vigorously, and working the little arms up and down in a way which perplexed Pat not a little. "We must get the little heart to work before we warm the little body, else the blood will run there and choke it, and it won't

"He seemed to have received no injury at all, and began to swallow the warm milk."—*Page* 120.

be able to beat again. Set the heart going first, and then we'll wrap him in blankets by the fire. That's what I have always been taught. And put the kettle right on the fire, sonny, and get the bath out ready. I do believe—praise the Lord!—that the darling is living still. If he is, and if he gets a bit better, a hot bath will restore him quicker than anything. And get that box of dried herbs and sea-weed from the cupboard. There are some rare good things there for rubbing the skin with. I've seen wonderful cures with them in my young days."

Pat was intensely excited as he watched his mother's quick and clever ministrations to the little boy, who already began to look different —less like a child of marble, and more like one of flesh and blood. It seemed very, very long to Pat before his mother looked up with kindling eyes to say he was still alive; but Eileen herself had been surprised at the quickness with which the little heart had begun to beat beneath her hands, and decided in her own mind that the child could not have been very long in the water before they saw him.

Pat ran from the kitchen, where his mother's

operations were carried on, to the little room
where Jim had been carried by Nat, and
reported to each worker the success of the
other. Jim very soon began to breathe again.
He was not in the state the child had been, but
he had evidently received some blow which had
injured him in some way Nat could not at once
determine. He awoke in great pain, and on
trying to move himself became again uncon-
scious; and Nat could only apply hot flannels
to the side where the pain seemed to be worst,
and get his wife, when she could spare the
time, to mix him some of her simples, which
had the effect of sending him off to sleep at
last.

The little boy's case was different altogether.
He seemed to have received no injury at all,
but to be suffering simply from exposure and
the length of time he had been in the water.
The bath of herbs and pungent roots prepared
by Eileen seemed to have a marvellous effect
upon him, and he began to swallow the warm
milk in teaspoonfuls which she gave him from
time to time, each time with increased ease and
eagerness.

"He likes it, mother," cried Pat excitedly;

"I'm sure he likes it. I do wish he'd open his eyes and smile. Is he asleep, or what?"

"I hope he'll be asleep soon," answered Eileen, as she dried him by the fire, and prepared to lay him in her own well-warmed bed. "He's coming round beautiful, and if he doesn't get a fever on it, which I'm in hopes he won't after what I've done for him, he may wake up to know us in another few hours. But he'll be best in bed now; and so would you, honey. You've been up the whole night long, my little son. Shall mother put the pretty little boy to bed first, and then little Pat?"

It had not occurred to Pat before that he was tired; but now he found that he could only just keep his eyes open, and that his limbs were quite stiff from fatigue. So after seeing the little stranger boy put to bed, he consented to be undressed and fed himself. "Just as if I were a baby myself!" as he said sleepily; and his head had hardly touched the pillow before he fell fast, fast asleep, and slept for more hours at a time than he ever remembered to have done in all his life before.

CHAPTER VII

THE LITTLE PRINCE

WHAT was that noise? Pat sat up in bed to listen; and as he did so, he began to wonder where he was, and what had happened; for he had an impression that there was something strange in the way the light fell on the wall, and in his mind there was a feeling that some great event had taken place which he could not at that moment recall; and then, what *was* that noise in the living-room? It was for all the world like the sound of a little child laughing and prattling; but how had any child come to Lone Rock in the night? . . . And then all in a moment, like a flash, it came back to Pat—all the events of the night of the storm, the dismasted ship, the little boy lashed to the spar, Jim's heroic attempt to save the child—everything that had occurred up to the time he had let his mother put him to bed in broad daylight. It was daylight again now. He knew by the place the sun had got to on the wall that it was not only day, but afternoon. He thought for a moment that it was the afternoon of the day on which he had gone to bed ; but he soon found out that it was the day following that one. He had slept for more than twenty-four hours, as little folks will sometimes do when they have been through great fatigue and excitement ; and now he waked up as fresh as a lark, and full of eager curiosity about the new inmate of the lighthouse.

He slipped out of bed, and into his clothes as fast as possible, and then stepped softly across the floor, and peeped into the next room. He wanted to see the little stranger before he was himself seen. He wanted to have a good look at him, and in this he was not disappointed.

The living-room looked very neat and trim. All the disorder and mess which had been brought in the previous day was cleared away. The table was spread for a meal, and Eileen herself was sitting comfortably in her rocking-chair, with a laughing little boy perched upon her knee, laughing and crowing lustily at the movement of the chair. He was a great many years younger than Pat—this little waif of the ocean—perhaps not more than four years old. He had quantities of soft yellow hair, that floated round his head like a cloud, all curly and pretty; and his skin was like a peach in its soft bloom and pretty rich colour. He had big dark eyes that seemed full of sunshine, and when he laughed his little teeth looked like pearls. Pat thought he had never seen such a wonderful and lovely little boy before. He himself was not handsome, though he had a dear little shrewd intelligent face of his own, and a pair of pretty grey eyes like his mother's. Indeed, Pat had never before troubled his head as to whether people were pretty or the reverse; but the beauty of this child struck him as something so wonderful, that he could not help noticing it, and rejoicing in it. He had not thought about it in that strange night when the little guest had been brought in, looking like a marble image on a church monument. It was hard to believe that this could be the same being; and yet, of course, it must be. He came slowly forward, almost timidly, feeling as though he must apologise for his intrusion to this fairy prince.

His mother looked up, and greeted his appearance with a smile.

"Well, honey, quite rested after your vigil? That is right. And if you are up, will you mind the little boy whilst I get the tea? We have been living a strange life these past two days, and I scarce know what to call the meals; but father will like some tea when he comes down; and Jim, may be, will take a cup, too. Poor fellow! I wish we could get a doctor to him, but I'm afraid there'll be small chance of that for a week or more. The sea will run so high after the storm, though the wind does seem to be going down at last."

For the moment Pat was too much engrossed with this wonderful little boy to heed even what his mother said of Jim. He was standing on his own feet now, where Eileen had set him, looking hard at Pat, as though wondering who he was, and where he had come from. He was dressed in a little old suit of Pat's clothes, which was many sizes too big for him, though

Pat had long outgrown them. Yet little figure of fun as he was in this respect, nothing could destroy the look of dainty finish and beauty which seemed to belong to him as by a natural inheritance, and after he had indulged in a good long stare at Pat, a smile beamed all over his face, and he remarked graciously—

"I'll play wis 'oo, ickle boy. I likes to play nice dames."

Pat was his slave in a moment, begging to be allowed to crawl round the room with the little prince on his back; and as this form of entertainment was mightily to the liking of the small guest, it was carried on uninterruptedly till Nat came down from the lighthouse, and laughed aloud to see the two children thus occupied.

"What! is he turning a little tyrant already?" asked the father, as he picked up the rider, and lifted him high in the air, laughing and shouting in glee at this sudden change in the game. "So, Pat, my boy, you are awake at last! We thought you had turned into one of the seven sleepers, whoever they may be; and this young man, too, though he woke up the first, and shows he has the making of a first-rate jack-tar in him. He's none the worse for

a wetting that would have made an end of
any landlubber. He must be cut out for a
sailor—aren't you, my hearty?"

The child laughed, and danced up and down
in those strong arms, and pulled Nat's beard,
and shouted with glee. He was certainly none
the worse, to all appearance, for the narrow
escape of his life. Eileen marvelled at him,
and her faith in her herbs and simples was ten-
fold increased. Perhaps Nature has secrets which
are better known to the humble than the learned,
for surely this unlettered woman, with her store
of half-superstitious lore, gleaned in her girl-
hood from old women who were learned in the
matter of Nature's cures, had achieved a result
that many a medical man would have envied
her. She was proud and delighted at her own
success, and could hardly believe that any child
could have gone through so much, and yet be
so well and hearty twenty-four hours later.

"He was never born to be drowned—the
little rogue—that's plain enough!" laughed
Nat, as he took his seat at table, and gave the
child to his wife. "And now let me have my
tea as quick as you can, for there is double work
up aloft since poor Jim is laid by his heels."

Pat stood beside his father, and waited on him with assiduity.

"How is poor Jim, and what is the matter with him? May I take him his tea? He will like it, I think, if I bring it."

"I think he will, sonny. He speaks of thee more than of any other. I scarce know what is the matter. It seems like as if he had broken a rib or two, and they were pressing inwards, somehow. He can't move without pain, and sometimes can scarce draw breath. But so long as he's lying still and quiet he seems fairly comfortable like. We must get a doctor to him as soon as ever we can. I've signalled ashore that we wan't help; but I'm afeard it will be some days before any boat can come anigh us."

Pat took the cup of tea and slice of buttered toast his mother had made, and went carefully with it to Jim's little dark room, which was not far away.

Jim was lying propped up with pillows, and there was a curious whiteness about his weather-beaten face, and a sunken look about his cheeks, which made Pat realise in a moment that he must be very ill. His heavy eyes, however, lightened at sight of the child, and he just moved his hand along the counterpane in token of greeting.

"I've brought you some tea, Jim," he said softly; "I'm going to stop and give it you. I'm a good hand with sick folks. Mother always says so when she's ill. You needn't move or talk if you don't want to. I'll do everything for you. You've been a hero, you know, Jim; and now we must take care of you till you're well. I wonder what it feels like to be a hero? Do you feel different from what you did before that night?"

Something like the ghost of a smile passed across the man's face, and he made a slight sign of dissent. Pat saw that he could not talk much, and he contented himself with giving him the tea, and coaxing him to try and swallow just a morsel of the toast, talking to him softly the while, and telling him how well and strong and beautiful the little boy was. Jim listened with evident interest and pleasure, but speech was visibly difficult, and the only con- nected words he spoke were whispered just at the end before Pat went away and left him.

"I want you to read. . . . Just a few verses

. . . about Peter . . . walking on the sea, . . . and what the Lord said to him;" and Pat understood in a moment, and got the Bible from the table, and quickly found the place.

As he read the simple story, a happy and satisfied look passed over Jim's face, and he closed his eyes as though he were asleep. Pat put the book back, and as he did so he could not help noticing how many signs of wear it showed, considering that it was new only a few months before; and there were bits of paper tucked into so many different places. It was plain that Jim had read it a great deal. Pat thought that it must have been that which helped Jim to be a hero that stormy night. The child knew he had risked his life to save the little boy, and he loved Jim with an admiring, re-verential love, quite different from his former affection.

But since there could be no conversation, he need not linger here, and he began to want his own tea, as well as the society of the beautiful little boy. Stealing from Jim's darkened room he found his way back to his mother, and there was his tea all ready for him, and the little boy enjoying his own share mightily, perched on Eileen's knee, and chattering away to her in a babbling fashion, which she seemed to understand better than Pat did all at once.

"Mother, what is his name? Can he tell us?" asked Pat eagerly; and the question being put by Eileen to the child, was received by a gurgling baby laugh, and an answer which the listening Pat barely understood.

" He calls himself Prince Rupert, by what I can make out," she said, turning with a smile to her own boy. " I've asked him again and again, for I don't know whether that isn't a pet name, not his own——"

"Oh, but, mother, why should it be? I'm sure he's a sort of little prince—one can tell it by looking at him!" cried the delighted Pat. " Prince Rupert! What a pretty name! Oh, mother, I have wanted so often to see a real live prince. Mother, are any of the Queen's children called Prince Rupert? Do you think he might be one of them?"

Eileen smiled at the simple good faith with which Pat asked this question, and also at the wonder she saw in the boy's eyes as they were turned towards the little guest, who was busily engaged in trying to reach everything upon the table, that he might better examine its properties.

"No, dear; he's a deal too young to be our Queen's son, and there isn't a Prince Rupert amongst them; but he's plainly some well-born little boy, even if he isn't a real prince; and we must try and find out who his parents are, and where he came from, so soon as a boat can come to us, when the storm is over. Somebody must be mourning him for lost; unless, indeed, those who belong to him have found a watery grave themselves. One cannot guess how he came here, except that it must have been from some vessel, either wrecked or in great peril. He has been washed overboard—that's plain enough; but whether or not the ship went down, we cannot tell. We shall have to try and learn; but he can tell us nothing, bless him. He doesn't seem even to remember much about being on a ship. It's as if the salt water had washed everything out of his pretty head."

Pat's face was full of eager excitement and purpose.

"Oh, mother!" he cried; "and if nobody

comes for the little boy—if his relations have
been drowned in the ship—may we keep him?
May I have him for a brother? You know
you've said sometimes you wished I had a
brother to play with. If nobody else wants
Prince Rupert, may he stay here in the lighthouse with me? I should be so very happy if I
might have him always. I would take care of
him. He shouldn't be any trouble to you. Oh,
mother, do say yes! I do love him so very,
very much!"

Eileen was smiling at her little boy's request,
but she did not give him any direct answer.
She set the child on his feet, and he promptly
ran across to Pat with a shout of glee; and as
the pair scrambled to the floor for a renewed
romp together, she watched them a few minutes,
and then said—

"Poor little boy; he's too young to miss his
mother yet, but I fear she may be in a terrible
state of fear for him if she be living, poor soul.
We must not think of ourselves, little son. We
must think first of others. We must send word
ashore about the little boy, and the police will
do all they can to find out who he is. I can't
but think he was washed off yon great steamer

that was labouring past us that stormy night; and both Jim and your father think and hope that she weathered her way round the point, and reached harbour safely. If that is so, we shall soon hear who little Prince Rupert really is, and his parents or friends will send for him. That will be best of all; for this would be a poor sort of a home for him to be brought up in. He's plainly been used to something very different. Princes don't live in places like this, my little son."

"No, I suppose not," answered Pat wistfully, "but I would have tried to make him so very happy!"

"Well, make him as happy as you can whilst he is here. May be it will be for a good spell yet. And never mind what happens afterwards. You will always like to think you made his visit to the lighthouse a pleasant one."

So Pat set himself with all his heart to the task of entertaining the little prince thus wonderfully cast upon his hands. It was not difficult to do this, for the wee boy was the merriest of little mortals, and took an immense liking to Pat from the very first. Very soon Pat began to understand his lisping prattle perfectly, and was delighted with his sharp observation, and little airs of baby importance and mastery. It was very plain that Prince Rupert had been used to plenty of attention and petting. He demanded both as a natural right, and soon had the submissive Pat completely under his yoke. Pat was to sit by him when he had his bath, so that he could splash him all over with the water, crowing with mischievous delight all the while. Pat was to come into the inner room, and see him go to bed, and sit beside him and tell him a tale ; and of course Pat was enchanted to do this, and would have told him tales till midnight, had not his little tyrant speedily gone off to sleep, holding him fast by the hand. Pat never thought of taking his hand away. He would have sat by the little bed all night sooner than disturb his small majesty ; but his mother came in and unclasped the chubby fingers, whilst she tucked the little stranger warmly up in his cot ; and then Pat found that he was rather stiff and cramped, though he hardly knew then how to tear himself from the side of his new playmate.

"Isn't he beautiful, mother?" he whispered softly, as he stooped to kiss the little roseleaf face. "Oh, mother, it must have been Jesus who sent Jim to fetch him out of the sea."

"Yes, Pat, dear, I think it must have been. Dear, bonny little lamb—he's one of the dear Lord's own little children."

"Oh, yes, mother! and Jim told me before he went that it seemed just as if the Lord had called him to go out into the sea—like as He told Peter to come to Him, you know. Jim is very fond of that story. I read it to him often. You know, mother, Jesus kept Peter from sinking in the sea, and I think He must have been with Jim, too, for the waves were so very, very strong. I thought he would never be able to reach him. But he did; and then you and father pulled him safe to shore—but I don't think you could have done it if Jesus hadn't been helping too."

"I'm sure we could not," answered Eileen with dewy eyes, as she turned away and took Pat's hand tenderly in hers. I often think that the dear Lord is walking over the sea on stormy nights, very near indeed to those who are in peril, if they could but see Him there. And Pat, honey, did you say that Jim felt that too?

Did he think that he was doing it at the bidding of the Lord Jesus?"

"Yes, mother, I am sure he did. I can't remember just what he said, but it was something very like that. I'm almost sure that Jim loves Jesus very much now. He's always reading about Him in the Bible you bought for me to give him. Why do you cry, mother? Aren't you glad that Jim is happier than he was? because I am sure he is. I think it makes everybody happy to love Jesus, and to like to know about Him, and think about Him."

"Indeed it does, my little boy," answered Eileen, bending to kiss him, "and it's thankful I am that poor Jim has come out of the darkness into the light. Go to him, Pat, and see if he is asleep, or if he is wanting anything. I must try and get the little boy's clothes mended to-night for him. They were so drenched and stained I had to wash them out in rain water, and get them well cleaned and dried. I must sit up till they are ready for him to-morrow, for I can't bear to see him running about such a little object as he is in your old things. His own mother would scarce know him, I take it. Beautiful, soft, warm clothes his own are—too good to be really hurt by their wetting. Run to Jim, dear, and see if you can do anything for him, and then come back and read to me. Father will have a long watch again to-night, and I shall sit up and take a spell with him by-and-by. We must all put our shoulder to the wheel and help him till we can get help here from shore."

CHAPTER VIII

ND you were the little boy that was taken out of the water, and poor Jim was the brave man who swam into the great big waves to save you!"

Pat was the speaker, and the beautiful little boy the listener. They were sitting together in the hot sunshine, just beneath the south wall of the lighthouse, well sheltered from the wind; and the sun was shining with all the brilliance that it sometimes can in early February on the south coast, though the sea tumbled and foamed beneath the strong gale which still blew steadily day by day, and cut off Lone Rock from the mainland. But the weather began to show signs of modifying. The careful keeper of the lighthouse had that day told his wife that he believed a few more days would see the end of this bout of rough weather. The glass was beginning to rise after its long period of depression, and this was the third day on which the sun had shone out brightly and bravely, tempting the two children out upon the rocks for several hours, in the brightest part of the day. By this time the two boys were the best of friends. They were not happy for a moment if separated. Pat took the lead in devising amusement for his small guest, and was in one sense of the word the leading spirit, yet it was the little prince who really ruled the pair, for his word was law to his comrade, who could have sat and looked at him, or listened to his merry prattle for hours. The little gentleman had a way with him which had captivated every heart within the lighthouse. Nat and Eileen were almost as much his slaves as Pat. He could twist any one of the three round his chubby little fingers, and this was plainly no new art to him. Those merry ways of his, half-coaxing, half-commanding, had plainly been practised before. He was no novice in the art of getting what he wanted, this beautiful little prince (as Pat firmly and fully believed him to be); and it seemed to Eileen a pathetic thing that the little fellow should thus be cast among strangers, and those of a rank in life so much humbler than his own, without being able to explain to them who he was, nor whence he had come, although in other ways he could prattle away fast enough, and tell little stories, too, in his own peculiar fashion.

Eileen had listened in vain for any illusions to his parents in his talk; but the name of father or mother was never on his lips. Once, when she asked him where mother was, he pointed vaguely out over the sea; but she could not make out whether he meant anything by the gesture; and the only relative he ever spoke of was "Auntie;" whilst he did not appear to be pining after anybody, but was as merry as a lark from morning to night; very different from what Pat would have been, even as a little child, if suddenly robbed of all those whom he had learned to love.

"I sometimes think the water has washed the memory of what went before clean out of his head," Eileen had said to her husband, in some disappointment at her failure to learn anything of the boy's history from him. "It seems strange he should have forgotten everything, such a quick, noticing little fellow as he is. He talks a little about a ship to Pat; but never seems to remember the people who were with him. I can't make it out. At his age, Pat would have been able to tell anybody where he lived, and what his name was, and who his father and mother were. It puzzles me altogether, that it does. And we want to send a message ashore when the relief boat comes. I'd have liked to be able to say who the boy was."

"Well, we'll say enough for his relations to know him by, if he's got any living claim to him, poor little chap. I suppose the children of the gentry, who always have a nurse beside them, don't learn to be as knowing and independent as our little ones, who have to fend for themselves so much sooner. Pat may be will find out something more sooner or later. He chatters away to him like a young magpie. The child looks a deal better since his little prince came. It's good for boys to be together. I'll not grumble if his folks don't come for him in a hurry. Look at them now; why, they are as happy as kings together—and a deal happier

than many kings, I take it, if all we hear of the
ways of the world is true."

The two boys were sitting in the hot sunshine in the lee of the lighthouse, and the tame
sea-gull was hopping about near to them, sometimes diving into a pool after a dainty morsel
that caught his eye, sometimes flapping his
wings, and uttering his harsh cries, which
seemed those of joy at seeing the sunshine
again. Pat was evidently telling a tale to the
little one of more than usual interest. The
little prince's eyes were fixed upon his face
with a look of wrapped absorption, his rosy lips
were parted, and his whole expression was one
of deep and undivided attention. He was in
reality hearing the story of the little boy who
had been seen a few nights ago, just as it was
growing to be dawn, floating on the water on a
broken spar; and of the brave man in the
lighthouse, who had swum out amongst the
great waves to bring him in safe to shore; and
Prince Rupert had been more fascinated by this
tale—told with all the graphic power of which
the youthful eye-witness was capable—than by
any other from Pat's store; and when at the
close he was told that he himself had been the

little boy, and that it was Jim who had gone into the boiling sea to fetch him out, he looked fairly bewildered at the idea, and turning his dark eyes towards the lighthouse behind, he looked up and down, and then asked—

"And where is poor Jim?—does he live here, too?"

"Yes, he lives here," answered Pat. "But he got hurt that night. He has to lie in bed. I go to see him every day. Poor Jim looks very sad and poorly. Father says he won't be better till we can get a doctor to him."

Little Rupert's eyes were wide with sympathy and interest. He was quite a kind-hearted little fellow, though he had been taught to think first of himself and his own wishes, as too many little children are, whether those about them know it or not.

"Did he get hurted coming into the water after me?" he asked, in a voice that was quite soft and subdued with surprise and thought.

"Yes, Prince Rupert, he did," answered Pat. "I don't quite know how it was; but there was a big black thing floating in the water, too. I saw it, and a great wave came and carried it right against Jim. I think it might have hit

you, perhaps, only Jim saw it coming, and
turned over so that it came against him instead,
and a big wave broke all over him then, and I
couldn't see what happened. But I know he
got hurt then, for after that he couldn't help
himself a bit; and father and mother could
only pull you both in, for Jim never let go of
you. And it seemed like as if you were both
dead at first. But mother took care of you,
and father took care of Jim, and you both got
better. But Jim has to lie in bed, and his side
hurts him dreadfully when he moves. But you
can run about and play. I'm so glad you
weren't hurt, too. Do you remember being
washed into the water?"

But the child did not answer the question.
He seemed to be watching the gull at his queer
play; but he was evidently thinking of something else, for he turned presently to Pat, and
said with a lip that quivered a little—

"I don't like Jim to be hurted in getting me
out. Where does Jim live?"

"In there," answered Pat, indicating the
lighthouse behind. "When he was well, he
helped father to take care of her—the big lamp,
you know, that you went to see last night. He

can't help now, because he's ill. But when he gets better he will again."

"I'd like to go and see Jim," said the child, suddenly scrambling to his feet. "I fink Jim must be a very good man. I'll go and tell him so."

"Yes, do!" answered Pat eagerly. "I'm sure he would like it. I tell him about you every day, Prince Rupert. He likes to hear about you, I know, though he can't talk hardly at all. You must talk to him. He can't say hardly anything himself. It hurts him so ; and mother says he mustn't."

"I'll talk," answered the little prince serenely. "I can talk very well, if I like. I've heard people say so, though they don't always understand when I do. Why didn't you take me to see Jim before?"

"I don't know. I didn't think perhaps you'd care to come. You see, he has only a poor little dark room, and you are a little prince." Pat's loving admiration was betrayed in every word he spoke, and in the glance of his smiling eyes. He thought Rupert looked prettier than ever with his golden curls blowing about in the breeze, and his little face, with the

peach bloom tanned by the kisses of the sun-
beams which had been caressing it these past
days. His own stylish little sailor suit had
been neatly mended, too, and had not suffered
so very much by the long immersion in salt
water. The child had an air of refinement and
sovereignty about him of which Pat's sensitive
Irish nature was keenly conscious. He felt he
could lay down his life for this princely child;
and understood very well now how it was that
real kings and princes in history had got
hundreds and thousands of followers to go with
them to victory or death. Sometimes before,
his mother's stories had puzzled him. He did
not quite understand how men had been so
easily led to fight against fearful odds. But it
was no puzzle to him now. The spirit of hero-
worship had entered into his being, and had
made many things plain that had perplexed
him before.

" If I am a prince, princes must be good," said
the golden-haired child, suddenly straightening
himself out, and looking at Pat with a new
expression in his eyes.. It was as if some
sudden memory were coming back to him—
a memory of something or somebody almost

forgotten hitherto.   Pat held his breath to watch and listen.   "I know that's right.   She said so. I remember quite well.   She said, 'If you are a prince, you must be a good one,' and she kissed me, and took me in her arms.   The sea was all shining over there, just like it shines now. Was it here she said it, Pat?"

Pat shook his head.   He was almost as curious as his mother would have been to know who the "she" was whose words the child has just quoted.

But the flash of memory did not seem to go farther, and after a moment's pause, Rupert went back to his former theme, speaking with his baby lisp, yet in words quite intelligible to Pat.

"Take me to see poor Jim.   I'd like to see him.   I'd like to tell him he's a good man, and that I'm very much obliged to him for pulling me out of the sea.   I suppose I should have been drowned if he hadn't got me out in time; shouldn't I, Pat?"

"Yes, indeed you would; I thought you'd be drowned as it was.   It seemed such a long time before they could get you both out.   Now I'll take you to see poor Jim.   I'm sure he'll be pleased, though perhaps he won't seem to be. Jim is rather a funny man; but he's very nice when you know him. You won't be frightened if he looks rather cross at you?"

"Nobody looks cross at me, except nurse, when she's in a bad temper," answered the child serenely. "And only babies and girls are frightened at things. I wasn't frightened when the gull pecked me—you said so yourself."

"No, you weren't, you were very brave," said Pat, in loyal admiration; adding, after a moment's pause, "Now come with me. I'll take you to Jim; but go quietly, in case he's asleep. Mother says he gets so little sleep at night. We won't awake him if he should be asleep now. This is the way, just up these little steep stairs. There are only four of them. Have you never been here before?" and Pat laid his fingers on his lips, and pushed open the door, and peeped cautiously in before he turned back to his companion.

"We can go in. He's not asleep. His eyes are open. It's rather dark, when you first get in, but you'll see better when you've been in a little while. Jim," he added, advancing into the bare little wedge-shaped room which had been

Jim's as long as he had been on Lone Rock,
"Prince Rupert wants to come and see you.
I told him to-day about how you went into the
sea after him. He thinks it was very kind
of you."

"Lift me on the bed. I can't see him properly," spoke the second visitor in imperious
tones, and Pat hastened to obey. The next
minute the beautiful child and the rugged faced
man were looking straight at each other with
mutual curiosity and interest; and after a few
seconds spent in this silent inspection, Rupert
put out his tiny hand and laid it in Jim's.

"I like you," he said deliberately. "I fink
you're a very brave man; and you're a very
good one, too. I shall tell my papa about you.
I fink he will make you one of his soldiers, or
servants, or somefing like that. He will like
you very much for coming into the water after
me. He likes men when they are brave. He
is very brave himself. I shall tell him to take
you away from here, and let you be always with
him."

Pat listened breathlessly to these words.
The little prince had never before spoken in
this manner at all.

" Have you got a father ? " he asked in eager accents ; but Rupert looked at him as though he scarcely understood the question.

" Have you got a papa, little gentleman ? " asked Jim, in his very low, faint tones, so unlike the old strong gruff voice that used to rise above the tumult of the winds and the waves.

" *Torse* I have," answered the child, almost indignantly. " I'll tell my papa about you. He'll like you because you got yourself hurted instead of me. My papa did that himself once. He got nearly killed, instead of somebody else. Mamma told me about it her own self. And the Queen gave him a cross for it. She showed it me. It wasn't so very pretty ; but mamma said papa liked it better than anything else he had. Perhaps when I'm a man, I'll get one for myself ; but mamma said they only gave them to very brave men. P'raps they'll give one to you, Jim. You're very brave, you know. When my papa comes home, I'll tell him about you. He'll come and see you then. P'raps you'll have a cross, too."

Jim smiled faintly, and stroked the small hand that lay in his palm, rather as he might

have stroked a delicate rose petal that had
floated to him from the sky. He could not
talk; but it was a pleasure to lie and look at
this beautiful child; and Rupert became all at
once wonderfully communicative. He plainly
took a strange and wayward liking to Jim, as
children will do sometimes to the most unlikely
people.

"I feel as though he belonged to me," he
remarked later on in the living room, as the
mid-day meal was going forward. "You see,
he got me out of the water; and I fink my
papa will take him for one of his soldiers,
because he's so brave. I'm to be a soldier
when I grow up. Perhaps I'll have Jim to be
my orderly. Papa has an orderly, I know. I
suppose he keeps his things tidy for him. I
fink I'll have Jim for mine when he gets better.
Why doesn't he get better quickly?"

"Because we can't get a doctor to him yet,
little gentleman."

"My papa would send one if you'd ask him,"
said the child, in the same rather magnifi-
cent way. "He can send anybody anywhere,
I know. He can do anything he likes. My
papa is a very great man."

"And where does he live, dear?" asked
Eileen breathlessly, realising for the first time
that, though the words father and mother con-
veyed no impression to the child's mind, he
had a very decided notion about his papa and
mamma, although he had never spoken of them
before to-day; but the question was beyond the
child's power of answering. He looked perplexed for a moment, and then said—

"They're going home—we're all going home.
They'll go home as soon as the big ship gets to
land. I suppose they've gone home already,"
and then he looked about him with wide-open
wondering eyes, filled with a vague distress and
perplexity; and glancing up into Eileen's face,
he asked—

"Is this home? Is this where they are coming to, by-and-by?"

"No, darling," answered Eileen quickly, the
tears springing to her eyes as she realised the
possibility that the child's parents had found a
different home from the one they had talked
about to their little boy. "Papa and mamma
stayed on the big ship; and if the big ship got
safe into port, they would go home when they
landed; and we will find out where they are,

and you shall go to them. Don't cry, little prince. As soon as ever a boat can come from shore we will find out all about it."

"I don't want to cry," answered the child, whose wondering eyes were quite dry. "I like being here. I like you, and Pat, and Jim, and the gull, and everybody. I fink I'll stay here always. My papa and mamma can come and live with us if they want to; and if they don't, I'll go and see them sometimes. I don't live with them ever—only now and then. I'd like to be a lighthouse keeper, with Jim to help me. I fink I'll live always with you."

"Oh, do, do, do!" cried Pat, clapping his hands, and running across to his little prince, he folded him in his arms in a long embrace. "I should be so unhappy if you went away. Now I am going to give Jim his dinner. Will you come and help me?"

"*Torse* I will. I like Jim. I'll help you take care of him till he's better;" and the pair went off together, carefully carrying Jim's light repast, while Eileen looked up in perplexity at her husband, and said—

"What does the little fellow mean?—and why doesn't he seem to care more for his parents?

He has never cried for them, or seemed to miss
them, and yet he knows all about his papa and
mamma, as he calls them. I cannot make it
out—no, that I can't—such a warm-hearted
little fellow as he is, too."

Nat shook his head slowly. The problem
was beyond him also.

"May be we'll find out some day. It isn't all
fine folks that get the love of their little ones.
Perhaps they're too fine to notice him, and
he doesn't love them as our little one loves us.
But plainly his father is a soldier, and a bit of
a grand one, too. I doubt there'll be no trouble
in making out who the youngster is, once we
get ashore. But if he belongs to them as have
no love for him, it will be a hard matter to let
him go, though we'll have to do it, I suppose."

Eileen sighed at the thought, but knew it
would be inevitable. Yet as the days passed
by, the child endeared himself to them more
and more by the singular devotion he suddenly
conceived for "poor Jim," as he invariably
called him. He was in and out of the little
dark room morning, noon, and night. He in-
sisted on taking Pat's place on the bed at meal
times, and feeding the patient with his own

tiny but capable hands.   A singular bond grew
up between the rough man and the two
children, one of whom he had risked his life to
save ; and in this way the days slipped by, one
after another, until the sea went down, the
waves ceased to dash themselves against the
reef ; and Pat came tearing down from the
gallery in wild excitement one morning to
announce to his mother the fact that the relief
boat was coming out to Lone Rock as fast as
winds and waves could bring her.

CHAPTER IX

HELP FROM SHORE

HE two little boys stood hand in hand on the rocks, waving their caps and cheering as the boat came dashing through the foaming waves towards the Lone Rock. The sea was still running high, but approach was possible to those who well understood what they were about. A man stood upright in the bow of the boat, boat-hook in hand, and every few moments he called out some word of warning to those behind him. As the boat neared the rock, the sail came down with a run, and the crew, taking to their oars, rowed carefully and cautiously towards the basin where a boat could float at ease, and where Nat stood, ready to render assistance when the craft should come alongside.

"Glad to see you well and hearty, mate," shouted the man in the bow, as soon as he was within earshot. "We've been anxious about the Lone Rock ever since you signalled for help. We were afeard some harm had befallen you. What's wrong with you here?"

"Jim's on the sick list," shouted Nat back, "can't stir hand or foot. Have you brought a doctor with you, mates?"

"Ay, ay, he's here sure enough, and other things too you may want if you've a sick man with you. Is he too bad to be sent ashore? What's wrong with him?"

"The doctor must tell us that. My wife thinks it's broken ribs. I'll tell you the tale when you get on shore. Steady there with the boat! Ease her a bit and hold her back. There's a big drift running in just here. So steady! Here she comes. Throw me the line, mate. Now she'll do. Keep her steady and fend off from the rocks. So!"

The boys, watching with eager eyes the advance of the boat, cheered aloud when it was safely drawn up in the little creek. The man in the bow, who was an old crony of Nat's, looked at the pair with an air of astonishment.

"Why, Nat, you've never raised another in this time!" he exclaimed; "I never knew you had more than little Pat over here. Where did the second come from? He doesn't look much like a child of yours. He looks as if he's come straight from fairyland, wherever that may be."

"From the sea-fairies, then," answered Nat, with a smile, "for Jim got him out of the water the night when the storm was at its worst. That's how he came by the blow which has laid him by the heels. But the boy never seemed a bit the worse after he came to. He's a wonderful saucy little fellow, gentry-born, as one can see, and as bold as a little lion. Have you heard aught ashore of a child gone overboard in the gale?" The men shook their heads, looking with keen interest at the little golden-headed fellow who was helping Nat to hold the boat, and looking as though everything depended on himself!

"Look alive, men!" he piped out in his high pitched voice. "Tumble out and get ashore! We've been waiting for you ever such a lot of days! Lend a hand, Pat, and hold her steady!"

Laughing and admiring, the men sprang

ashore, speaking kindly words to Pat, whom
most of them knew, and looking with keen
interest at the beautiful little boy, who continued to issue his baby commands in such
nautical language as he could command.

" He's been afloat before now," said the men
one to another. " He's picked up that air from
some bo'sun as keeps his men well in order.
He's a rare young game-cock, he is! Picked
up out of the sea, was he, Nat? We must try
and find out where he comes from. Anything
about him to say?"

" No; and the spar he came on was not
picked up either. That might have told us
something; but it was so heavy Jim cut the
child loose before we hauled them both in.
There's a sort of a mark on some of his under-
clothes which my wife takes to have been a D
before it was well nigh washed out; but it's
hard to tell anything now, and all we can get
from him is that his name is Prince Rupert, and
that his father is a soldier. He seems to know
very little about his parents, and the salt water
perhaps washed most things out of his head.
He hasn't talked but very little of anything he
knew before; but he's a bold, merry little chap,

and will make a fine sailor one of these days.
Doesn't know what fear means!" The men all
looked with interest at the little waif, who was
busily engrossed with the rope—making fast the
boat, as he plainly believed—and ordering Pat
about in the most lordly way. His yellow curls
were blowing about his rosy face; his big dark
eyes were alight with excitement and self-im-
portance. No one could fail to regard the little
prince with admiration ; and the sailors laughed
together, and told Nat he had done a good thing
for himself in befriending such a boy as that.

"He comes of fine folks—any one can see
that, and they must be real set on such a smart
little chap as him," said one, as they began
to make their way to the lighthouse, where
Eileen stood in the doorway smiling a welcome.
"You won't be the loser by being good to him.
He's a fine little fellow, and no mistake !"

"So he is," answered Nat, "but I don't want
nothing for doing my duty by him. It was Jim
as risked his life to save him. If his folks
want to do something for him, I'll only think it
right and proper, since I doubt if the poor chap
will ever be the same again. But I've done
nothing, and I want nothing. My wife's had

L

all the bit of trouble he's been, and she'd do the same for any child that breathed, be he never so poor."

"Ay, that she would," answered more than one voice heartily. "She's a real good one is Eileen;" and then there were pleasant greetings between the bright-faced wife and mother and those who had come to assist the prisoners upon the Lone Rock; whilst the young surgeon, whom the sailors had brought with them, asked to be taken to his patient without more delay.

The boys lingered down by the boat, for the little prince was fascinated by it, and Pat had to show him everything, and explain the use of the various parts.

"We had boats," said Rupert, with his head a little on one side; "but they were fastened up so high I could never see into them. I like this boat. Do you fink we could get in and sail her off round and round the rock till the men want her again?"

But Pat negatived this bold suggestion, and Rupert was reluctantly borne off in-doors "to see how poor Jim was getting on," as Pat coaxingly put it, for he was quite afraid the daring little fellow would really try to cast the boat loose and let it drift away. Nat's knots would most likely prove too much for him; but there was no knowing what his determination might not achieve.

The doctor and Eileen were with poor Jim, and the men sat round the table partaking of the meal she had prepared for them, and hearing from Nat the whole history of the storm, and the details of the rescue of the little stranger, which was thought a very interesting piece of intelligence. "We'll do all we can to find out who he is when we get ashore," said the cockswain of the boat, "and we'll leave Robin behind to help you with the lighthouse till something can be settled. You've had a hard time of it, Nat, these last ten days—Jim laid up, and another little 'un on your wife's hands."

"My wife's a jewel," answered Nat, a smile beaming over his honest face. "She's the sort of helpmate for a man like me. Never a word of complaint, however hard the work, and she's always ready to take a watch and let me get a good sleep. Then luckily there was nothing went wrong with the light, and the days were clear and fine. It might have been a good bit worse; not but what I'll be glad enough to have

Robin's help for a spell. I fear me it'll be many weeks before Jim is up to anything again."

"Poor chap, I'm afeard he's a good bit hurt," said another, "but he seems a bit quieter like now. I wonder whether the doctor will let him be took ashore. He's a good bit of trouble to your wife here."

"I san't let Jim be took away," remarked a small voice from about the level of the table; "Jim's my pal. I likes him very much. I tell him tales, and I make him better. I san't let anybody take him away till my papa comes and makes him into a soldier, and then p'raps I'll go too, and everybody here, and we'll all live together somewhere where there's just a little more room. It isn't always just very con-wen-ient," with a gulp over the long word, "to have water everywhere all round. I fink a garden is better for some fings."

"Did you have a garden where you came from, my little man?" said the cockswain, lifting the child on to his knee amid a general laugh.

" *Torse* we did!" answered the child, looking up into the weather-beaten face fearlessly, "a great big garden, with trees and fings, and I

played there every day. It was nice ; but we
hadn't got a sea-gull there, only two dogs. I
fink I like a sea-gull best. He makes such nice
noises and he dances, too. I fink I shall dig a
great big ditch all round the garden, and fill it
with the sea, and put a lighthouse in the middle,
and Pat and his daddy and my Nan can live
with me there ; and the sea-gull, too, and then
we should have everything, and it would be
quite con-wenient for everybody."

" Do you know the name of the house where
you lived, my hearty ?" asked the man, with
beaming face ; but Rupert shook his head impa-
tiently, and went chattering on about how his
future domain was to be arranged.

" You can come sometimes in your big boat
and see us, man," he remarked, " and I'll show
you how to sail it in our sea, for I don't expect
you'll know how to do it properly. I shall have
a boat of my very own then : my papa will give
me one. And when I'm not a soldier I shall be
a sailor, and I'll teach you how to be one too."

" Thank you, my little man, I'll be sure and
come and learn of you," and the child looked a
little offended at the general laugh from the rest.

" You needn't bring those men with you

another time," he said, "I don't fink they understand fings properly."

At that moment the young surgeon reappeared
with Eileen in his wake. She looked grave and
sorrowful, and went to the fire to take off the
soup she was preparing, whilst the men glanced
up at the doctor, and asked what he thought of
his patient.

"We heard him groaning a good bit at first,
and Jim isn't one to cry out for naught," said
Rupert's friend; "I'm afraid he's a good bit
hurt. What do you make of him, sir? Can he
be taken ashore?"

"No, he must stay where he is. He could not
stand any sort of move yet. He has been badly
hurt, and there is a great deal of inflammation
about him.   He will be easier now that I have
bandaged him up right, and his lungs will have
a chance of healing; but he has been left much
too long without medical aid. If I could have
seen him at once, things would have been much
better. However, we will hope for the best.
Any way, the worst of the pain is over now, unless the inflammation spreads."

"Have you hurted my Jim?" asked Rupert,
doubling his little fists and bristling up like a

young turkey-cock. "If you have, I'll frash you. I won't have my Jim hurted. He came into the water after me. Now I'm taking care of him. You didn't ought to have gone and seen him without my leave!" and he strode up to the doctor as though he meant to inflict condign punishment upon him forthwith.

But the young man understood children, and soon made friends with the young autocrat, now ruling Lone Rock with a rod of iron. He soon got him to talk of himself, and called up many reminiscences of his past life, all of which he carefully noted. From his own better knowledge of the way in which gently-born children lived, he succeeded in eliciting more information from the boy than any of his other new friends had done.

When the little fellow grew tired of talking at last, and went out with Pat to play, the young man made some notes in his pocket book, and turning to Eileen, said—

"Are you anxious to be rid of your young charge? I will take him home to my mother if you like. I am sure she would give him shelter for a time, till he can be traced. Is he not rather a burden to you here?"

"Oh, no, sir, thank you kindly all the same; but unless it's wrong to say so, we's far rather keep him here till his own relations come for him. He's got that into our hearts that he almost seems like one of our own, bless him; and though I know the life's rough, and not what he's been used to, it hasn't seemed to hurt him."

"Hurt him! I should think not!—do the little rogue all the good in the world! There's nothing like roughing it a little to make a man of a boy brought up in luxury. Lone Rock discipline will be good for him in more ways than one. I was only thinking you would be rather full here with your patient and this boy, as well as the extra man left to help your husband; but you know best."

"Oh, the little fellow takes no room. He shares Pat's bed, and the two play together and help me with poor Jim, and I think they'd pine if they were took from each other now. Thank you kindly all the same, sir. Did you make out from the little boy who he was or where he came from?"

"Not exactly, but I think it's plain that he's been separated from his parents for some while, and that his father is either an officer in the army, or else holds some important official position in India. The child has been plainly made to understand that he is a very great man, and lives in kingly state somewhere. I think I have found out enough to help materially in identifying the boy when we set about to find out his belongings. He appears to be an only child of wealthy parents; and there will be inquiries after him along the coast, even if it is only for some trace of the drowned body. He could not have been so very long in the water before you got him, or he would have been more difficult to bring to life. It has been a wonderful escape, look at it as you will; and I hope that those to whom he belongs will do something for that brave fellow who risked his life for him ; for I greatly fear he has received an injury which will disable him from active labour for the rest of his life. It is difficult to tell so soon, but I have my fears that it will be so. I will come over again in the course of a week and see him, if it is possible. Meantime, you can only go on as you have been doing, and I hope, now the bandaging has been done which was so much needed, that he will be easier. I

see you are a very good nurse, and I leave him
in your hands with every confidence."

"I will do what I can for him, sir, I'm sure;
for he is a brave man, and he went to what
might well have been his death without a
thought for himself. But it's a hard thing to
be laid aside at his age, especially since he has
no friends to go to, and no relatives to help him.
He's had a very lonely life of it, and a hard one,
has poor Jim. It seems as though it was to be
hard to the very end."

" We will hope there are brighter days coming
for him," answered the young surgeon cheerfully;
"I shall certainly make it known, if we succeed
in tracing this child, that Jim has received these
injuries in saving him from certain death. I
cannot believe he will be allowed to suffer in
consequence—suffer any sort of want, I mean.
Poor fellow, he has had suffering enough of
another kind, and may have more still, though
I hope what I have done will give him ease."

And then the doctor went down to the boat
where the crew were by this time waiting for
him. The children were there, too, and cheered
lustily as the boat put off into the big waves
beyond the little creek. Rupert had stoutly

resisted the blandishments of the cockswain, and had quite declined to let himself be taken from "his Nan," as he had called Eileen almost from the first. He was in charge of the light-house, he gravely asserted, and he couldn't possibly go away unless his father came for him. He was very busy every day, helping to keep the light burning, and taking care of Jim. He was far too important a person to be spared, and he flatly refused to be taken away by anybody.

"Now we'll come and tell Jim all about it," he said, as soon as the boat had grown small and insignificant in the distance ; and as Jim was looking rather better by that time, he was pleased for Rupert to climb upon the bed and tell him all that had been said and done.

"They wanted to take you away, but I wouldn't allow it," said the little autocrat ; "I said you'd like better to stay here, and that I'd frash anybody who took you away. I san't let you go to anybody except my papa, and if he takes you we'll all go and have a lighthouse of our own somewhere else, where there isn't so much water. I fink it's a pity to put them in the middle of the sea; they'd be more con-wenient in a garden where we could get at them more easily.   We'll have our lighthouse in a garden when we go away from here.

Then Pat stole in with his soft step, and Jim looked at the Bible that lay beside him, and Pat took it and read a story, and explained it to Rupert as he was used to do now.   The little boy liked this wind up of the day almost as much as Jim, and was always very attentive.

"I'll say my prayers to Jim to-night," he remarked suddenly, when the reading had concluded, " because I fink he's a very good man. I want him to get quite better, so we'll ask Jesus if He won't make him.   I fink He must love poor Jim very much ! "

CHAPTER X

A WONDERFUL DAY

HE two little boys were up in the gallery. Nat was burnishing the reflectors and overlooking the great She, whose wonderful individuality was taking a strong hold upon the imagination of both the children. Rupert knew almost all Pat's stories about the wonderful creature who slept all the day, but waked up to keep watch all the night, and he was never tired of watching her cleaned and fed ; but the process lasted longer some days than others, and they would vary the morning's work by going out upon the sunny gallery, and calling out to the men at work within what vessels were in sight, and where they seemed to be going. And whilst thus occupied, Rupert would generally demand that Pat should tell

him some of Jim's many stories, many of which
they would try to enact between them, making
believe that the gallery was the deck of a ship,
and that they were the officers in charge. Pat's
vivid imagination, inherited from his mother,
made this kind of make-believe easy and en-
trancing to him, and Rupert delighted in it, and
in flourishing about and being the lord and
master of everything and everybody. He was
growing so brown and sturdy that it was a treat
to look at him, and Pat had increased in health
and strength visibly since he had had a little
playmate to romp with. Before that he had been
inclined to spend rather too much time in sitting and thinking. The sea and the rocks and
the sky gave him many strange ideas; and
there was Jim, too, who wanted so often to
know things that took a great deal of puzzling
out. Pat had liked all the thinking, being of
a cogitative turn, but it was better for him to
run about and shout and play more, and to sit
and ponder rather less. The parents looked in
wonder at him sometimes, remembering how all
last winter he had seemed wasting away, and
had fallen into a state from which it seemed as
though nothing but a miracle could lift him.

They could not be thankful enough for the wonderful change. The dreamy wistfulness which had lingered so long in his eyes, was changing now to something more boyish and healthy. He did not look as though he were always walking on the border-land of the unseen world. The romps and merry games with his little companion were fast making a boy of him again, and Nat looked with hearty satisfaction at the change.

A merry rosy pair they were up aloft to-day, and their shouts of glee rang cheerily over the dancing water. Eileen now and again heard them as she sat at her needle below, and she would smile and glance upwards, as though to try and see what the urchins were about. To-day was a glad one at the lighthouse, for Jim had taken a decided turn for the better. Now that the broken ribs were properly set and in place, and no longer pressing upon the organs they had injured, he was relieved of the worst of the pain. He had been able to sleep and eat better, and to-day he felt so strong that he had coaxed Nat and Eileen to let him get up and sit beside the fire in the living room, well wrapped up in blankets, and with plenty of rugs about him. The doctor had said he might do this if he felt well enough, as a change of posture might be a relief. The children had watched the move with great interest; but had been sent upstairs after a while to let Jim rest and be quiet. The mother had told Pat to go and look out whether any boat from shore might not be coming to the rock. It was a fine day, and the week had expired which was to bring the doctor for another visit. He might come any day now; and the children were delighted to go up aloft and play the game of "look-out man," as they called it.

There were a good many fishing boats out in the bay, and Rupert had been certain that every one of them was coming to Lone Rock, till at last he had grown weary of watching, had declared that nobody was coming to-day, and had suggested another game at which they had played some time. When, however, they were tired of this, Pat had gone to the rail to look over, and now he called to Rupert with some excitement.

"Come and look! Come and look!" he called out, "I do believe that boat is coming here! Look how she skims along! What a pretty one she is! How white her sail is!

And doesn't she go fast! I don't know that boat, Prince Rupert. I don't think she belongs in the bay. Yet she looks just as if she was coming here. Shall I call father and ask him what he thinks? She doesn't turn or tack. She comes straight, straight on. Oh, I do hope she is coming! Perhaps she has got something for you on board."

"Perhaps it is my papa come for me," said Rupert, not looking as though he knew exactly whether he relished this thought or not, "but I'm not sure that I'll go away with him if it is. I like being here. I like playing lighthouse games. I didn't have anybody to play with me before. I don't much fink I will go with him if he comes. I fink I'll belong to you're father and mother. I like them very much."

Pat, not quite knowing how to reply, and greatly moved in spirit in case this pretty white-sailed boat should be coming to rob them of their darling, hastily called his father, who came out into the bright sunshine, and shaded his eyes with his hand.

"It looks as though she were making for Lone Rock," he said, "and it's no boat from

M

our bay, Pat; it's a better built and better-rigged
craft than we often see in these parts. It's a
yacht's boat by the look of her, and a tidy little
craft she is. Well, well, we shall soon know;
but she's heading for Lone Rock as sure as fate;
and it's not the coast-guard inspection, neither.
That boat belongs to some gentleman, I'll be
bound," and the man's eyes turned towards the
little fellow beside him with a look that Pat
understood in a moment. His eyes filled with
tears, and for a moment everything swam in a
golden haze. They were coming to take away
his little prince, the darling little boy who had
become the first object in his life. However
should he bear to let him go? It did not do to
think about it. If he thought, he would surely
cry, and that would be a pity, for perhaps Rupert
would cry too, and it would never do for his
parents to find him in tears, they would think he
had been badly treated, and take him away as
quick as thought. No, he must put a brave face
on, and try to make the best of it. Perhaps
Prince Rupert would decide not to go, and Pat
could hardly believe that his word would not be
law if he once boldly asserted his determination.

" Shall we go down and watch her come in, and tell her how to make the creek?" he asked of the child, and Rupert assented gladly.

Nat, too, descended the winding steps with the two children, and as he passed out he said to his wife—

" I believe the little fellow's friends are coming for him, wifie. There's a boat on its way that doesn't belong to our parts. Make the place as bright as you can, and set some food on the table. I'll make them welcome to come in if they have a mind. May be they'll like to see the place as their little boy has lived in these last weeks."

Eileen's kitchen was always neat and trim, and she soon whisked out a bright table-cover, and a few bits of ornaments, to smarten up the place, as she did for Sundays and holidays, or when summer guests were expected. Jim still sat by the fire dozing, and scarcely alive to what was passing ; but it was out of the question to think of moving him again so soon. There he was and there he must remain ; but she cast a quick eye all over her small domain, and saw that everything else was in order ; and then she

went out to see what was happening outside.

The children were standing below on the
rocks, for the tide was ebbing, and nearly low.
The sun caught the yellow curls of the little
prince, and made them shine like gold. He
was visibly excited, and kept hopping from one
foot to another, whilst Pat held his hand in a
close, protecting clasp, and kept him from slip-
ping in his excitement, and falling amongst the
wet sea-weed.

Nearer and nearer came the pretty boat,
skimming its way through the water like a
white-winged sea-bird. It was manned by
sailors in uniform; plainly it was what Nat
had said, the boat from some gentleman's yacht.
"That's our boat, I do believe!" cried little
Rupert, as it drew near. "Our men wear fings
like that on their heads. I fink papa must have
sent them to fetch me!"

Pat's heart beat so fast he did not know
how to reply; but there was no need for him
to say anything; for just at that moment the
sail came fluttering down; they saw in the
stern of the boat a lady and gentleman, sitting
together, looking eagerly ahead; and the next

"'That's our boat, I do believe,' cried Rupert."—*Page* 180.

moment a cry went up that awoke an answering thrill in Eileen's heart, and made the tears spring suddenly to Pat's eyes—the cry of a woman's voice—

"It is! It is! Rupert! Rupert! My own little boy!"

Rupert started at the sound of that call, looked hard at the boat, and then waved his little hand joyously.

"Mamma! Mamma!" he cried, and pulling Pat by the sleeve, he added, in a tone of pleasurable excitement, "That lady is my mamma, Pat, and the gentleman is my papa, and those are his sailors. I should have liked him to bring his soldiers better; but perhaps he has them on shore waiting." Pat looked as one in a dream. He could not understand it—the child's calmness in the recognition which should have filled him with ecstasy, and the evident deep emotion of the mother. Hardly had the boat touched the rock before the pretty young lady, with the sweet, sad face, had sprung out, catching at Nat's outstretched hand, and in another moment she had come flying towards them, and sinking on her knees upon the wet sea-weed, she took the little one in her arms in a clasp so close that it seemed as though she would never let him go ; and Pat knew that the tears were raining down her face, and that the reason why she did not speak was that she could not for overmastering emotion.

When he looked up it was to find a tall, stalwart, bronzed man standing beside them, who put his hand upon Pat's head, and said kindly—

"Well, my little man, and have you been helping to take care of our little boy for us all these days?" and Pat crimsoned to his very ears with shyness and pleasure.

"We are all so very, very fond of him, sir," answered the boy shamefacedly. "Are you going to take him away from us?"

He could not help asking the wistful question, and as he did so he raised his face and met the glance of a pair of very kindly, though very keen eyes fixed upon him. The question seemed half to amuse and half to surprise the gentleman, who hesitated a moment before he said—

"Don't you think that is what is our business to do, since he belongs to us, eh, little man?"

"I—I suppose so, sir," answered Pat sorrowfully, " only we shall so miss him when he is gone ! "

" Well, well, we will see, we will see," said the gentleman kindly, and then he stooped over the child, and said in a voice which shook just a very little in spite of the playful ring in it—

" Well, Rupert, my little boy, haven't you got one word or look for papa ?—or have you forgotten him altogether ? "

" I haven't forgot — *torse* I haven't — but mamma frottles me so ! " answered the little fellow, who was by this time trying to wriggle himself free from the embrace of his agitated mother, which had become too close for comfort. He seemed better pleased when his father took him up in his strong arms, and he laughed and kicked with pleasure, as he did when Nat took and tossed him high in the air.

The lady rose from her knees, wiping from her eyes the tears which still seemed inclined to start, and putting out her soft hand to Pat, she said very gently and sweetly—

" And so you are the little boy who has been playing the part of brother to our dear little Rupert. Have you got a kiss to spare for me, my little man ? "

And Pat felt hot all over with surprise and pleasure, as the gentle, beautiful lady bent her head and kissed him, and he hardly dared to kiss her back, lest it should be taking a liberty; but he remembered that queens had their hands kissed when they sat in state, and so he raised the white hand that held his to his lips, and kissed it reverently.

"Shall I take you to my mother, madam?" he asked. "She has taken care of Prince Rupert. I only played with him and helped her."

"Prince Rupert!" repeated the lady, smiling. "Who taught you to call him that?"

"He said Rupert was his name," answered Pat, looking up, "and we all know he must be a little prince—he looks so like one."

The lady smiled again, her tears were drying now. Eileen had come forward by this time, and had heard the last words. The lady stepped forward, and held out her hands to the light-house-keeper's wife.

"I have heard of your goodness to my boy," she said, in a quivering voice, "how can I thank you for it?"

"I do not want any thanks, my lady,"

answered Eileen, with her soft shy pride. " I
would have done the same for any blessed
baby cast up on our shores; and the darling
has won his way to all our hearts—and it's
a real prince of princes that he is—the bonny
boy ! "

" No, no—not a prince at all—only a very
spoiled little boy, I am afraid," said the mother,
with something between a sob and a laugh.
" A little boy who badly wants his father and
mother's care and training. But we had to
leave him with my sisters when we were sent
out to India in haste two years ago ; and we
have been there ever since. He was brought
out to meet us as we came home ; he came
in my husband's yacht, which met us at Malta,
and we were to come home to England in her.
The child had hardly more than learned to
know us well before that fearful night, when
we thought we must go to the bottom before
we reached port. Oh, how can I tell you the
agony we suffered when we heard that the
mast to which the child had been lashed for
protection had been snapped clean off, and had
gone overboard, and we running before the
gale as our only chance, and expecting almost

moment by moment to be sucked beneath the cruel waves! It only seemed then as though he had been the first. There was water below, and above the waves swept the deck every moment. I was lashed to another mast; but I was almost insensible from cold and exposure. I think I saw the light of the lighthouse above us as we passed half a mile off from it. I had just heard then that the child had gone, and nothing seemed to matter then, whether we lived or died. And then somehow we got round the headland, in the wake of a big steamer also in distress, and they helped us, though in need of help themselves, and at last we both weathered the storm together. But, oh! what days of misery those were when we thought we had lost for ever in this world the little son we had just received back after those long years of absence!"

Tears of sympathy were in Eileen's eyes; but she began to understand many things that had puzzled her before.

"Oh, my lady, I am so thankful to hear you speak so. I was grieved that the little boy spoke so little of you, and seemed to care so little whether his own father and mother came for him or not. Glad was I for sure that he was happy with us ; but it didn't seem natural-like for him never to pine a bit for his mother. It made me afraid (you'll forgive me speaking so plain) that his parents had not cared for him as a child should be cared for, and that went to my heart ; but now——"

"Ah, yes, you understand how it was—we had only had him with us for a bare ten days—and part of that time he was sea-sick and fret-ful, and could scarce be made to look at us. It was only the last few days that he was his bonny bright self, learning to love us and know us. No wonder he forgot us quickly after that fearful night. I cannot think how he lived in those boiling waves. Oh, I must see the brave man who saved him ! The doctor who came over with us in our boat has told me how he injured himself in plunging after our darling. Oh, you must tell us what we can do for him—what we can do for you all—to show our grati-tude. I did not know how to believe it when Mr. Deering told us that our little boy was alive and well, and very happy on Lone Rock in the care of the keeper of the lighthouse ! "

"Bless him ! He has been as happy as the

day is long, and he and my Pat have played like brothers, if you will pardon my boldness in saying so."

"Nay, what is there to pardon ; are they not brothers in the sight of our God?" said the lady, with a sparkle of tears in her eyes. "If you only knew what it was to me to hear how he had been cared for—my little boy, whom we were mourning as dead! Ah, you must let us be friends after this," she added, turning her sweet quivering face full on Eileen. "I cannot and I will not talk of 'rewards' to those who have shown themselves the best and truest of friends to my child, when only devotion such as he received could have saved his precious life. It would be a wrong to you and to me ; but you must let us be your friends from this time forth. You must let us see what may be best done for your happiness and his. *You* saved his life by your skill and promptitude when he was brought ashore, as much as the brave sailor did who plunged into the waves to bring him out of the water. You must never think that I could forget that."

"Oh, my lady, I only did what any other mother would have done——"

"Ah, but you did more than some *could* have done, because you had skill and knowledge beyond what many have. The doctor said so himself. But let me see the sailor who saved my child. I must thank him, too. And he must never suffer for his devotion in risking his life for our boy. You must tell me what I can do for him. Mr. Deering says he fears he will never be strong again."

"Oh, I don't know, my lady. He is getting on ; but he hasn't tried to do aught but sit by the fire yet. But he's up to-day, and you can see him by stepping indoors. May I just tell him you are here ? But I do not know by what name to call you ? "

"I am Lady St. John," was the answer. " My husband is Sir Arthur St. John, who—but you will hardly know that. And Rupert is our only child. Let me go and see the man who saved his life."

Eileen was sadly afraid that Jim would be very rough and gruff when the visitor came and stood beside him ; but somehow—whether it was that illness had softened him, or that the influence of the children had had an effect upon him, or that the inherent sweetness of the lady took effect in an unexpected manner—anyhow, he was wonderfully gentle in his manner to both the strangers, and though he said almost nothing, his rugged face looked smiling and peaceful, and there was no rough turning away from the kindness that was proffered. Not much was said that first visit; but a great many questions were asked both of the Careys and of Jim. The visitors sat down to partake of the simple fare provided for them, and whilst they ate they talked and asked questions. Eileen, intent on hospitable cares, scarcely noted all that was passing, and Nat was too straightforward and unsuspecting to see the drift of much that was said, and spoke freely enough in reply to Sir Arthur's various inquiries as to his past life, his qualifications, tastes, and pursuits. Pat's health was also mentioned, for it had been for his sake that his father had ever consented to become an inmate of Lone Rock Lighthouse. And whilst the elders thus talked, Pat and Rupert sat close together, and sometimes Pat had to brush away the tears from his eyes, for he knew the parents would take their little boy home with them, and it was dreadful to him to think of seeing his little prince no more. Rupert, too, was very

much divided in mind as to whether or not he
would "let himself be took away;" but Pat
loyally told him in eager whispers that he must
"do as his own mother wished," and the tie of
blood was beginning to assert itself when once
the little fellow had felt his parents' arms around
him.

But when the moment for parting came, and
Lady St. John saw the tears in the eyes of Eileen,
and the manful struggles on Pat's part to keep
back his sobs, her own eyes looked very dewy,
and she turned and spoke quickly in a foreign
tongue for several moments with her husband.
Then turning to the expectant group on the
rocks, she said, smiling sweetly—

"You will see us all again very soon. I
promise to bring Rupert back to see you in
about a week's time from this—at least if we
get a fine day. So cheer up, my brave little
Pat, and do not cry, Mrs. Carey. You shall see
your nursling again very soon; and I hope we
may have pleasant news for you by that
time."

Then the lady stepped into the boat, Nat took
the boy from his wife's arms and handed him to
his mother, half eager and half reluctant to go,

N

Sir Arthur followed, and the men pushed off, whilst Pat watched through a mist of tears the disappearance of his fairy prince, who seemed for the moment to have vanished out of his life for ever.

CHAPTER XI

THE PROMISED VISIT

AT lived in a chronic state of excited expectation after the departure of little Rupert, counting the days till the week should be over, and then spending almost all his time in waiting and watching for the white-sailed boat which should bring his little prince back to him again.

But for this hope to look forward to, the child would have felt very keenly the absence of his playmate; for they all sadly missed the happy laughter and baby prattle of the golden-haired child they had learned to love. Jim seemed to miss him as much as anybody, and perhaps both he and Pat were happiest when sitting over the fire together after dusk, and talking of his beauty, his bold, masterful ways, and the quick, clever things he had said and done. They never seemed tired of the subject, and if Pat was not reading to Jim out of the book they both loved so well, they were almost always talking of Rupert, wondering where he was, and what he was doing, and whether he would come soon and see them and Lone Rock again.

Poor Jim only got on very slowly. The doctor who had come with Sir Arthur and Lady St. John in their boat had told them it would be a long time before he would be fit for any sort of work again, and Jim began to feel as though his working days were over for ever. He had of late lost flesh and muscle rather fast. He noticed how shrunken his arms began to look, and Pat would sometimes tell him that his face was much thinner than it used to be. His bronze was paling too, and now that Eileen kept his hair neatly brushed and trimmed, and his bushy beard was reduced to order, he certainly looked a very different creature from the rough, uncouth Jim of past days. He used to feel a sheepish sort of pride when Pat would hold up a little looking-glass before his face to show him "how handsome he was getting!" But certainly the change both in the man's

aspect and the expression of his face was greatly
in his favour; and Eileen found it hard to
remember that she had once thought him the
most rugged specimen of humanity that she had
ever come across. But she was more and more
convinced that there was something seriously
wrong with him, and that he would never be
able to resume the hard life of a seaman which
he had always led hitherto. What would become
of the poor fellow she could not bear to think,
only that the recollection of Lady St. John's
gentle look and words would occur to her at
intervals, and she felt sure that the lady would
not allow the brave rescuer of her child to
come to want through his act of devotion and
bravery.

What Jim thought about it all himself she
did not know, until one night when they chanced
to be alone together whilst the other men were
up aloft, and Pat was sleeping soundly in his
bed. The wind had been rather wild again the
last few nights, and it was blowing half-a-gale
now. Eileen was preparing something hot for
the watchers when they should come down, and
Jim, who was not disposed to go to bed just yet,
was sitting watching her.

" It must seem a strange sort of thing to you, Jim," she said, smiling, " to have naught to do with the lamp on nights like these. I wonder if you miss going up to her (as Pat says) these nights? Do you think of her or dream of her in your sleep ? "

"Now and again I do—dream I'm going up and up and up the stairs, and can't never reach the top. That's the nights when my breathing's bad. It comes to me like a dream of going on and on up the stairs, not able to breathe, and the stairs never ending. I'm glad to wake then, and find myself in bed. Sometimes I wonder whether I'll ever get up those stairs again."

Eileen's face was full of sympathy and quick comprehension.

"Do you feel like that, Jim? Do you feel very bad ? "

"I don't know rightly how to say it; but I feel as though all the life and spring had been took out of me. I don't seem to have no strength inside nor out. That's all I feel. The pain don't trouble me much. But I've a feeling sometimes that it could be pretty sharp if I was to try moving about or lifting weights again.

I don't know whether I shall ever get up those stairs to have a look at her again. Sometimes I feel as if my last look would be when the boat comes to take me away from the Lone Rock for good and all."

"Oh, Jim! But you're not going to leave us yet!"

"I don't know, my lass. I don't know. But I'm only a useless log here, and any day they may send and fetch me away. I sent a message by the doctor to them on shore, saying as I wasn't able to do my work, and that I couldn't look to stay on here. I've sort of expected to be took away ever since, but they haven't come for me yet."

"And where will you go, Jim, when they do take you ashore?" asked Eileen, with wide-open, wondering eyes. "Have you got any friends as would give you a bit of a home till you were fit for work again?"

"Nay, I've got naught of that sort," answered the man quietly. "You see I wasn't never one for making friends at the best of time, and the last ten years I've been in prison, or else here on Lone Rock. I suppose they'll take me into the 'Firmary till I'm a bit stronger and better;

and if so be as I'm never fit to earn my bread again, I suppose I shall get kept on there the rest of my time."

"Oh, Jim!" cried Eileen, her eyes full of tears, "you don't never mean you'll have to spend the rest of your days in the workhouse!"

He shook his head gently, and his face grew strangely soft and thoughtful.

"Nay, lass, I don't know—I can't see not a step before me; but somehow that don't trouble me. May be it's because I'm weak-like and sick; but the thought about what's coming doesn't trouble me one bit. I've a feeling somewhere that the Lord will see after me; and His way is sure to be the best, and will lead straightest home. It seemed like as if He called me by name that night, and I went out into the sea not knowing whether I'd sink in the waves or not. He kept me from that, and brought me safe ashore, and it seems as though I could leave everything else to Him now. I couldn't see the way in the dark, with the waves all tumbling and washing over me; but He could see, and so He can now. That's how I think about it; it's all right as long as He knows."

Eileen's tears dropped, but she turned her

face away and dried them quickly, and then her smile shone out like a sunbeam.

" Well, if that's how you feel about it, you're a happy man, Jim, and I needn't worrit myself about you as I have been doing. If we only leave the future in the hands of the blessed Saviour, we never find that He gives us cause to regret. He cares for us a deal better than we know how to care for ourselves."

" It's caring for ourselves as makes us sink in the waves, I'm thinking, often," said Jim thoughtfully. " 'That was the way with Peter. It was all right with him so long as he looked at the Lord and trusted. It was only when he began to think about himself, and the danger he was in, that he began to sink, and then so soon as he cried to the Lord he was saved, and helped in the midst of his peril. It all comes to that all the Bible through—do the best you can— do the duty that comes to you—and leave the rest to Him. That was in my head all the while that night. I can't feel afraid now. Whatever comes to be will be His doing."

And after that Eileen ceased to fret herself over poor Jim's future. She felt that he had within him that which would brighten his lot, and make it a happy one, be it cast where it might.

The seas ran too high for several days longer for there to be any hope of a visit to Lone Rock, but towards the end of the month a calm came down on the face of the sea, and Pat resumed his watch with the greatest eagerness and interest. How he wished that Jim could climb up to the gallery and share it with him, but Jim was quite unable to think of attempting such a feat. So the little boy divided his time between the high look-out place and the fireside where Jim passed his time; and Eileen spruced up her kitchen, and made it as bright as hands could make it, to be ready day by day for the arrival of the little prince on his promised visit.

One day Pat saw a beautiful yacht steaming past the Lone Rock at half a mile distance, and making for the bay beyond. He was always interested in such a vessel, but he did not connect her appearance with the return of his little prince, till he presently saw her casting anchor in the bay and launching a boat from the side; and then in great excitement he got his father to come with the telescope, and five minutes later was tearing down the winding stairs at the risk of toppling down and breaking his neck in his haste.

"Mother! mother! Jim! — he's coming! They're coming! I saw them quite plain. They came in a beautiful ship of their own, and now the boat is coming to the rock. Oh, mother! they are all there—the king and the queen and the little prince"—for so Pat was accustomed to speak of them, in spite of his father's laughter and his mother's attempted explanations. "Oh, Jim, do come down to the rocks and see them land! Prince Rupert will be so pleased to see you there. Come, mother! Come, Jim!"

There was no resisting him. Jim could hobble about a little with his stick, and the three went out together into the bright sunshine, and stood watching whilst the white-winged boat came skimming over the waves towards them. Pat was wildly waving his cap, and shouting out his greetings long before they could be heard ; but as soon as the boat got within hail, the little yellow-haired boy, who was in a suit of sailor white, and a veritable picture of childish beauty, sprang up in his seat and began waving his straw hat, and shouting

at the very pitch of his voice, and hardly had
the boat touched the rocks before the two
boys were in each other's arms, hugging and
kissing as though they never meant to let each
other go. The mothers stood looking on and
smiling, Eileen half ashamed at the "forward-
ness" of her child before the gentry, but Lady
St. John, all smiles and sweetness, as she turned
to her, and said—

"My little Rupert has been crying out for
Pat every day, and sometimes will not be pacified without him. I am so glad for them to
meet again. I think you made him happier on
Lone Rock than we have done at home."

"Oh, my lady, don't say that!" said the
woman, half pleased, half shamed, as she led
the way within, Rupert leaving Pat for a
moment to give her a warm hug, and then
dashing at Jim to renew acquaintance with
him.

"We must manage for them to be friends
still," said the sweet-voiced lady as she entered
Eileen's bright living-room, whilst the men and
the children remained outside. "It is not good
for children to be brought up without com-
panionship, and Pat is such a dear, gentle,

little fellow, Rupert will learn nothing but
good from him."

"I hope he will learn no harm, my lady; but
Pat is only a sailor's son, and I hope he will
not take liberties with the little gentleman. It
was being so much together those days that did
it, but——"

"Now, you must not speak as though I were
not very glad my boy should make a friend of
your son," said Lady St. John, in her sweet
way. "I know that in after life their paths
will lie widely asunder, but that is no reason
why as children they should not play together,
and love each other. And it will do my child
good to learn, whilst he is still young, that
the lives of others are not cast in quite such
pleasant places. It will give him sympathy
and comprehension as to the troubles of others,
which it is right that all should learn. And
now, Eileen—if you will let me call you by
your pretty name——"

"Please do, my lady. Most folks call me so.
I know myself best by it."

"Yes, and I have heard so much about you
by that name that it comes first to my lips. So
Eileen, then, I want you to sit down and talk

with me a little about the future. Now that
Pat's health is re-established, are you still
anxious to remain upon the lighthouse? Is
Lone Rock the home you would choose for
yourself if you had the choice?"

"Well, no, my lady, I can't say it is; though
we have been very happy through the best part
of a year. It's a lonely life, and a rough one,
and there's no way of getting the boy taught,
save what his father and I can teach him ourselves, and we should like him to be better
educated than we were. But I'm afraid if we
took him back where he came from, he would
droop and pine again; and the pay here is
good and regular, and the work not so very
hard, save in rough weather. Still——"

"Still, if anything should turn up that would
give you a pleasant country home, and advan-
tages for Pat, without all the drawbacks of the
lonely lighthouse life, you would be willing to
think about it?"

"Why, yes, my lady," answered Eileen, smiling, "glad, and thankful, too. But chances
like that seldom come to us poor folks; and we
must not repine, for we have been very happy
here."

"I am sure you have," answered the lady, "but my husband and I want you to be happy somewhere else instead. I will tell you in a few words what has recently happened to us. The death of a relative has put us in possession of a large property on the coast a few miles to the eastward of Lone Rock. This has made my husband give up his position in the army, and come home to live. The yacht which met us at Malta with our child is another possession of his, and the sailing-master, who has been in charge of her many years now, and has come in for an annuity from our relative, is anxious to retire when his place is filled. My husband wants your husband to take command of the yacht. He has made all due inquiries about him, and is satisfied that he is qualified for the post. We shall not use it a great deal, but we intend to keep it, as our means allow it, and we are both fond of the sea. You would have a cottage on the estate to live in—most likely one of the lodges—and your husband would be a great deal ashore as well as a good deal afloat, and there is anchorage for the yacht quite near to the Hall, which is on the coast, as I have said. Pat could go to school, and would still have sea air about him, and a pleasant country home to live in; and as for poor Jim, he is to receive a pension so long as he is in any wise disabled, and we should be very glad to pay you a fixed sum for boarding him out with you, as there is plenty of room in the lodge, and he could help to open the gate even before he was able to take any other employment, which we shall find for him when he gets stronger, as I trust he may——"

But Lady St. John stopped short there, for Eileen had suddenly thrown her apron over her head, and was sobbing aloud.

"You are not distressed, I hope?" began Lady St. John; but Eileen, by a great effort, recovered herself, and looked up with brimming eyes that were shining like stars through the mist of happy tears.

"Oh, my lady, my lady! it seems too good to be true; sure they are tears of joy I am shedding. It's myself that can hardly believe my own ears. I don't know what to say, nor how to thank you. It's like a blessed dream entirely—that's what it is, and my breath is fairly took away!"

"Oh, if that is all, I do not mind," said the

lady, smiling; "tears of joy are soon dried. Well, Eileen, I believe my husband and yours are talking it over outside now; and I hope by what you say that he will be willing to entertain the offer. I have set my heart upon having you and Pat at the lodge, and then my little Rupert will not quite lose his playfellow. The children will be able to meet and enjoy a game of play together sometimes, and, perhaps, as Pat grows up, if he takes kindly to his father's life, he may live to take his place in time, and remain as my boy's captain or mate, when his parents' sailing days are over. Rupert must never forget what he owes to those who saved him from death that fearful night. I think that that is a story which will become engraved upon his heart, as it is engraved upon that of his mother."

A sound of voices without warned the women that others were coming in. Nat entered with a happy glance beaming from his eyes, and an expression of mingled bewilderment and delight upon his face.

"Have you heard the news, wife?" he asked; "I scarce know whether I am standing on my head or my heels."

O

"And you will take it, Nat?" asked the wife breathlessly, and Lady St. John waited eagerly for the reply.

"Take it? Ay, that I will, and be thankful to them who offer it, and to the good God who watches over us. I don't like this rough life for you and the little one. We've had a good winter this last year at Lone Rock, and you've made home home to a man, even out here. But it's not the right place for a woman and a bairn. I've been thinking so more and more as I've heard sailors tell of some of the hardships that have been lived through here. The boy has got his health back again, thank the Lord, and we've been happy here, and I'd not have thrown it up in haste if nothing else hadn't come in the way. And I'll not be in a hurry now to leave them before they can get another man to suit. But we'll not turn our backs on such a chance as has come in our path. I've told Sir Arthur that I thank him most kindly for thinking of us all like this; and since we may take poor Jim ashore with us, and make a home for him still—why, there's not another word to be said. We'll be ready to go ashore as soon as they can get a man to

take charge of the Lone Rock. I can't say
more than that."

"And that is quite enough," answered Sir
Arthur, smiling; "I would not have you act
unfairly by your employers, and my sailing-
master will remain on with me till you are free,
and for a little while longer, to show you the
ways of the vessel. And now, that being all
settled, we will think of getting away from
here; but it will not be long before we meet
again, and then our boys will not find that
visiting each other is fraught with quite so
many difficulties."

Rupert was a good deal displeased at being
carried off so quickly, but the parents knew
that those on the rock would have too much to
discuss to wish their visitors to remain. The
little autocrat was pacified by hearing that Pat
and Jim should come to see him at home quite
soon, and whilst the boat sailed away in the
distance, Pat was told the wonderful news,
whilst Jim sat still on the rock which was his
usual seat out of doors, and gazed out over the
sparkling water, his hands clasped together on
the top of his stick, and his chin resting upon
them in meditative fashion.

"Oh!" cried Pat, when he fully understood the whole matter; "isn't it wonderful? Isn't it just like a story, mother? Oh, Jim! what do you think about it?"

"Why, it seems to me," answered the man quietly, "for all the world as though the Lord had done it. It's just His way of helping us out of the deep waters, and it's too good not to be true."

CHAPTER XII

HAPPY DAYS

T was a lovely evening in August. The sun was setting in a blaze of splendour over the sparkling sea. The smooth shaven lawns and majestic sweep of park land around the fine old Tudor house were looking their loveliest upon an evening like this, and down by the sea, just where the creek ran up through a belt of woodland, and into the very garden itself, a man and a boy were waiting beside a neat little boat, fitted with cushions and other requisites of comfort, as if in expectation that somebody from the great house behind the trees would shortly be coming down for an evening row or sail.

The man and the boy were both dressed in suits of sailor blue. Their caps were of the same pattern, and had in gold letters round them the words, " Prince Rupert." The same words were painted in gilt letters upon the pretty boat; and the little boy—who was none other than Pat, only grown wonderfully brown and healthy and strong-looking—sometimes glanced at the name with a smile, and then up at Jim's smart head-gear.

"This is better than Lone Rock, isn't it, Jim?" he said, breaking the silence which had lasted some considerable time. "We didn't think last summer ever to be in a place like this."

"No, that we didn't," answered Jim, with the smile, which was now so frequently seen, and which lightened his rugged face wonderfully. "It's a better place than ever I dreamed of once; though I know now there's a better one still waiting for us by-and-by."

Jim's face lighted as he spoke with a look that Pat was used to seeing there now, and which always filled him with a certain wonder and awe. Jim had been up and about again for some little time now. He had the sole charge of the three boats which were kept in the boat-house in the creek, and used by the people in

the big house whenever they wanted a sail or
a row. No more scrupulously clean and attentive boat-keeper had ever been known, and all
who came to the house noticed Jim, and had
a kind word for him. But it was already quite
plain that the man would never be fit for hard
work again. He had received an injury on the
night of the storm which baffled the skill of all
the clever doctors who had been called in to see
him. They could "patch him up" for a little
while; they could give him sufficient ease and
strength to enable him to get about his light
daily tasks with comfort and pleasure. He
could sail a boat in the bay in fine weather, or
gently scull the light little *Prince Rupert* about
with its young master as passenger. But that
was about all he was fit for, and those who had
heard the doctors' verdict knew that any winter
he was liable to be carried suddenly off through
the injury to the lung, which had so nearly
caused his death whilst he lay in the lighthouse
under the care of Eileen. Jim knew this himself as well as any one, but the thought gave
him no trouble or anxiety. He was wonderfully
happy and contented in his life; yet he was as
ready as ever to go forth over the unknown sea

if the Lord should hold out His hand and bid him come.

"Do you miss *her* very much?" asked Pat, after a pause, turning his eyes towards the sea in the direction of the Lone Rock, which in very clear weather could be distinguished from the garden wall. "You were fond of her, and knew her better than the rest of us. Do you think she misses you now that you're gone?"

"Why, no, I hardly think she do," answered Jim, with a smile; "I'd got into the way of thinking and speaking of her as though she were alive—it seemed a bit of company when one was all alone. But when I wasn't alone any more, why, she didn't seem to be more than a big lamp then. I always look out for her of a night when the light shines over the sea, but I don't seem to want to be over there no more. It's wonderful how one grows to like the life one has to lead. I used to think I'd never be happy off Lone Rock, and now——"

"I know you're happy here, Jim," said Pat, with a quick upward glance of loving admiration; "you always look so happy!"

"I oughter to be ashamed of myself, if I wasn't," said Jim. "If I was a prince I couldn't

be better took care of, and me able to do so
little. It 'ud make me ashamed, it would, if
our lady wasn't the sweetest mistress that ever
drew breath. It does one good to see her face
day by day. It's like a bit of God's sunshine
come down on earth—that's what it is."

" Yes, I do love her, and little Prince Rupert
too," answered Pat eagerly. " Oh, Jim ! what
a thing it's been for us your swimming into the
sea that night and pulling him out. It hurt
you a great deal, I know ; but you're glad you
went, aren't you ? "

Jim's face wore a look that it often did when
his thoughts were growing beyond his powers of
expression. It was some little time before he
tried to speak.

" Yes, Pat, lad, I'm glad enough I went ; but
I'd have been just as glad, I hope, if it hadn't
brought none of these good things to us."

" Do you mean you'd have been glad if you'd
had to go to the workhouse as mother was
afraid once ? " asked Pat, with wide-open eyes ;
and Jim looked at the boy with a curious half-
smile in his eyes.

" Well, I suppose the Lord Jesus is with His
folks in the workhouse as well as anywhere else,

Pat, and if so be as He's there, I can't think it could be such a bad place. I know old folks make a deal of fuss against going there, and may be it's right to struggle as long as one can to earn a living oneself; nay, I'm sure it is. But if so be as He sends sickness, and there's nothing else for it, why, I suppose He'll be there to take the sting away, like as He does always. I don't think folks think quite enough about that when they talk agin the workhouse. It's the way we get into of thinking all about ourselves and scarce a bit about Him."

"That's not your way, Jim," said Pat warmly; "I think you're always thinking of Him."

"I've got so much lost time to make up, you see, Pat," answered the man gravely; "I'd never thought of Him, and of all He'd done for me, till you brought it back to me again. I've lived the best part of my life without Him. It's wonderful how He'll take the poor bit that's left, when all one's best years were spent in forgetting and scorning Him."

Pat looked grave and said nothing. The thought was rather beyond his comprehension, but it always made him happy to think that he had helped Jim back to the light, though he never quite knew what he had done.

A joyful sound close at hand caused both the pair to start, and a little figure in white darted forth round an angle of the path, and yellow-haired Rupert stood before them, his face beaming with delight.

" Good evening, Jim ; good evening, Pat ! I'm going to have a beautiful row to-night, and mamma's come to see how well I row. See, there she comes through the trees ! Lift me in quick, Jim, and you come too, Pat, I want her to see how well I do it. Let me have the sculls. I can do it like a man now ! "

Jim was already in the boat, and helped the eager little boy in, where he stood between his knees, with his hands upon the sculls, which Jim was getting ready for use. Pat sprang after and took the tiller, pushing off from shore just as the lady came round the angle of the path to nod to them with sweet smiling glances.

" Look, mamma ! Look at me, mamma ! I'm sculling ! " shouted Rupert, his bright face all in a glow of importance and pleasure, " I can scull as well as Jim now, and I'll take you out sometimes like papa does, when I've got time. But

I like going with Pat and Jim best. It's like as
if we were living together in the lighthouse and
had just gone out for a row."

"Yes, darling," answered the mother, smiling
and waving her hand. "Take good care of Pat
and Jim, because they took good care of you
once. How are you feeling to-day, Jim? and
how is your mother, Pat?"

"Nicely, thank you, my lady," they both
answered in a breath, and the lady waved her
hand once more to the party before turning
back towards the house again.

"She knows you are safe with me," remarked
Rupert, slightly transposing a phrase he frequently heard from his parents' lips, and then
the boat was headed towards the Lone Rock,
and Rupert played the game all the time that
they were living there again. He and Jim and
Pat had been across once with Nat since their
coming to live at the Lodge, and Rupert never
forgot that it had once been his temporary
home, and made many plans about buying it
for his very own when he was a man, and
going there to live with Pat. Whenever he had
little friends of his own to tea at home, he
would always assert his superiority over them

by telling how he had once lived in a light-house, which certainly none of the others had done. And the story of his life there never failed to arouse a great interest and wonder.

The child's father was waiting to take him when the boat neared shore again, and he spoke kindly to Jim and Pat before leading his little son home.

As the latter put away the boat safe in the boathouse, and walked slowly towards the pretty lodge together, they saw the light from the Lone Rock streaming out over the darkening water, increasing every moment in brightness. Pat looked lovingly at it.

"I used to wonder as I lay in bed how she would look to people a long way off. I didn't know she was quite so bright. I think they must be taking good care of her, Jim."

"Yes, I think so, she's bright enough of nights. I can just see her as I lie awake in bed—through that gap in the trees. It makes me think about the Lamp to our feet and the Light to our path."

" Oh, yes," answered Pat quickly and eagerly, "that's what mother said too, Jim, and she said something else as well; I wonder if I could

remember it. I think it was about you. I
know it made me think of you directly she
said it."

"About me?" questioned Jim absently, his
eyes still on the light.

They had paused now upon a little bit of
rising ground to look over the sea. A short
distance to the right, a little bit farther up the
hill, twinkled the lights from a charming little
lodge, within the rose-covered walls of which
Eileen was stepping to and fro setting out the
supper, whilst Nat smoked his pipe by the
handful of fire, looking the picture of contentment and well-being. Pat could see the lights
from both his past and present home as he
stood beside Jim on the brow of the rising
ground, waiting till the man should have recovered breath to go on, for going up hill
always tried him a little, even though he went
slowly. But it was their habit to stand thus a
few minutes looking out towards the lighthouse,
especially after dark, when the rays of the lamp
could be seen ; and now Pat took up the word
again and went on eagerly—

"Yes; mother was saying that when she
looked out at night and saw the light, and the

great track it made in the water, it made her think about some words in the Bible, where it says about the ' path of the just shining more and more unto the perfect day.' And when she said it I thought of you, Jim, and I said to mother, 'Isn't that what Jim's path does, mother?' And she said, 'Yes, Pat, I think it is; because Jim seems to me to be going on more and more to the perfect day than anybody I ever saw before.' So it must be like you, Jim, for mother always knows."

Jim made no response in words; but Pat saw him draw his hand softly across his eyes. Presently he laid his hand upon the boy's shoulder, and there was something in the touch that made Pat look suddenly up. He met a glance of such affection and tenderness that for the moment he felt half startled, and then Jim spoke in tones that faltered a little with the deepness of his feeling.

" You mustn't think too well of me, Pat; you don't know what I've been through in the dark before the light came. I'm the last man in the world as should be spoken of so. But I do know that my sins are washed away. I do know that He's taken the burden off my back. He's led me into the light now, and I think He'll keep me there to the end. But, Pat, is was you're little hand that first pointed the way. I can't see how I should ever have found it if the Lord hadn't sent you to show it me. There's never a night as I lie watching the light, and thinking of that other Light that lighteth every man that cometh into the world, if so be as he'll turn his eyes towards it, but that I think of those old days of black darkness, when there wasn't a ray of light in my poor heart. And then I think of how the light came, and how He sent it to me. For it must have been His doing all the while that you came to Lone Rock, Pat, and taught me to know that we were never alone if so be as we would take the Lord at His word, and go to Him across the blackness and the darkness."

THE END.